SHAKEN UP

Also by Alex Morgan

THE KICKS

saving the team

sabotage season

win or lose

hat trick

BREAKAWAY: BEYOND THE GOAL

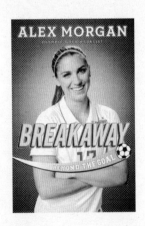

ALEX MORGAN

Simon & Schuster Books for Young Readers
New York   London   Toronto   Sydney   New Delhi

SIMON & SCHUSTER BOOKS FOR YOUNG READERS

An imprint of Simon & Schuster Children's Publishing Division

1230 Avenue of the Americas, New York, New York 10020

SIMON & SCHUSTER BOOKS FOR YOUNG READERS is a trademark of Simon & Schuster, Inc.

For information about special discounts for bulk purchases, please contact Simon & Schuster Special Sales at 1-866-506-1949 or business@simonandschuster.com.

The Simon & Schuster Speakers Bureau can bring authors to your live event. For more information or to book an event, contact the Simon & Schuster Speakers Bureau at 1-866-248-3049 or visit our website at www.simonspeakers.com.

Book design by Krista Vossen

The text for this book is set in Berling.

Manufactured in the United States of America

0715 FFG

2 4 6 8 10 9 7 5 3 1

CIP data for this book is available from the Library of Congress.

ISBN 978-1-4814-5100-0

ISBN 978-1-4814-5102-4 (eBook)

FIRST EDITION

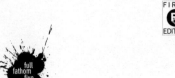

SHAKEN UP

CHAPTER ONE

Coach Darby's whistle shrieked. "Interception! Great job, Devin!"

I beamed. "Thanks, Coach!" I called back. We were on the soccer field at Pinewood Rec Center, practicing with my winter league team, the Griffons.

The regular school soccer season was over until the spring, and I'd been going into serious soccer withdrawal until my friend Jessi had suggested we try out for the winter league. Some of us on the Griffons were students at Kentville Middle School in Kentville, California. We played soccer for the Kentville Kangaroos, or the Kicks, as most people called us. When the Kicks' season had ended, I'd been crushed. But now I was back on the field doing what I loved most!

I passed the soccer ball I had stolen during our scrimmage to Jessi, who in turn kicked it to Kelly. I was teamed up with Jessi, Kelly, and Zarine. We were squaring off against Mirabelle, Lauren, Sasha, and Tracey. The rest of the Griffons were watching us as they did some basic dribbling on the sidelines.

"I want to give everyone a chance to touch the ball," Coach Darby said before she broke us into smaller groups. Scrimmages are practice games between members of the same team. Most of the time we scrimmaged with the whole team. Today was different. It was only 4 on 4. No one in goal, so each team's defender had to keep an eye out for scoring threats.

"All four of your teammates must touch the ball before scoring, or else the goal doesn't count," Coach Darby said.

That meant we all had to kick the ball before trying to make a goal. So Kelly kicked the ball to Zarine, who sent it back my way. Since all four of us had handled the ball, I was ready to go for a goal. But Mirabelle swooped in and stole it from me. Coach Darby's whistle sounded again. "Nice work, Mirabelle!"

The other team had possession. Lauren passed the ball to Mirabelle, who passed it back to her. Lauren eyed Sasha. I moved in, but the ball skirted just out of my reach before Sasha had possession. She sent it to Tracey, and I once again narrowly missed it. Tracey sent the ball to Lauren, but her shot was a little wide. This was the moment I'd been waiting for. I intercepted the ball. Focusing on accuracy, I kicked the ball to Kelly, who sent it back to me. I passed it to Jessi, who swooped in, narrowly missing an attack by Mirabelle. Jessi lobbed it to Zarine, who scored.

"Nice work!" Jessi high-fived me as Coach Darby's whistle blew.

"Everyone over here!" Coach barked, and the Griffons, who were on the sidelines, came running over.

"Time for the shooting gallery!" Coach Darby shouted with a little smile on her lips.

Her announcement was met with half the team groaning and the other half clapping. Coach Darby's version of a shooting gallery drill was fun, but it was pretty exhausting, so it was always met with a mixed reaction. That was why Coach, who didn't usually smile much, had a small grin on her face.

"You're up first, Devin." Coach pointed to just outside the penalty area, where she had placed the ball.

The drill involved lots of running and shooting, which was pretty intense, but I loved it. The object was to try to make goals from several different spots in the goal zone, running from one point to another as quickly as possible. Teammates would pass a ball to the shooter at each spot. Each player tried scoring goals not just from different places but in different ways, such as kicking it in or heading it in.

I started by taking a basic shot into one of the corners of the goal. Then I had to sprint to the penalty spot and shoot a ball.

For my next attempt, Jamie was waiting to pass a ball to me, and she sent it a little wide, so that I had to run to get it. When I looked up at her with an annoyed expression on my face, I saw her smirk. Yeah, I realized, she had totally done that on purpose. (Jamie had never really liked me.) But I kept going, racing to one side of the goal box and heading into the net a ball tossed to me by Coach Darby.

As fast as I could, I ran to the other side of the goal box and waited for Katie to toss me a ball, which I also headed into the net. Then I was racing back again to the penalty spot, where Jessi was ready and waiting. She passed a soccer ball to me, and I shot it into the goal.

"Good control, Devin!" Coach yelled as the next up, Kelly, took my place.

As I watched Kelly run through the routine I had just performed, I took a minute to catch my breath. I was panting hard.

After Kelly finished, she came walking over to me, breathing heavily, her hands on her hips. She threw herself onto the grass at my feet.

"That was brutal," she moaned dramatically.

I laughed. Kelly was one of the toughest players on the team, and I knew she could take it. She smiled up at me and laughed too. I was amazed at how much things had changed. When the winter league had begun just a few weeks before, the other members of the Griffons hadn't been very friendly. Everyone had been ultracompetitive and focused on themselves. Soccer was a team sport, so that meant we hadn't been playing very well to begin with.

But once we'd broken the ice and everyone had gotten to know one another, not only had practice become more fun, but we'd also started winning. Coach Darby, who was all about competition, even among her own players, had loosened up a bit too.

After the last of the Griffons finished up the shooting drill, Coach had us cool down by walking around the field and doing some stretches. "Great practice, everyone. Way to hustle! See you tomorrow."

Everyone started to walk off the field, until Jessi yelled, "Wait!" Heads turned as my friend waved everyone back. Jessi was definitely not shy. "We forgot something!"

Coach Darby frowned, but Jessi kept going. "The team cheer! We said we would figure it out today, remember? We've got a game on Saturday, and we have to get the cheer ready."

Squeals filled the air.

"Fun!"

"I've got one!"

"Let's do it!"

Even Coach Darby smiled. "Let's see what you got, girls."

Everyone gathered together, excited to share their ideas, except for Jamie, who looked back at us, rolled her eyes, and kept walking to the parking lot. On the Kicks we had competed against Jamie and her school team, the Riverdale Rams. Jamie played dirty and had even masterminded a plot to sabotage the Kicks. She had been seriously unhappy when she'd found out she and I were on the same winter team together, and she had taken it out on me on the field. But once the Griffons had started gelling, nobody had wanted to put up with her bad behavior anymore. She mostly kept to herself now, which I counted as a win. Anything was better than her pushing and stealing the ball from her own teammates!

With Jamie gone I knew that coming up with a cheer would be a total blast, with no one to put us down for having fun. I turned to the group, with plenty of my own ideas, as Sasha asked, "What about 'Olé'?"

As soon as the word was out of her mouth, all of us started singing the popular soccer anthem.

"Olé, olé, olé, olé, olé," we chanted along together, jumping around with silly smiles on our faces.

When we finished, Katie chimed in with an idea. "How about, 'Let's go, let's fight, Griffons gonna win tonight!'"

She ended it by throwing her hands out in front of her, her palms out and fingers spread wide. "Jazz hands!" she said with a laugh.

Everyone laughed along with her and tried to add their own silly dance moves to the mix. Jessi grabbed her foot and bent her leg at the knee behind her. Balancing on one leg, she began to turn in a circle, with her other arm behind her head, moving her elbow back and forth toward her face. "The Sprinkler!" she shouted.

Soon we were all doing the Sprinkler—some better than others. A few of us face-planted on the soccer field, yet I managed to hold my own. None of us could stop laughing, even those of us who wound up eating grass.

Coach Darby's loud "Ahem!" brought us back to reality. "I don't think the Sprinkler or jazz hands are what you're looking for. You need something to motivate you and get you pumped up for the win," she said, all business, as usual.

"How about 'I Believe'?" I suggested. It was one of my favorite soccer chants.

This suggestion was met with immediate approval. We all got together in a huddle, arms around one another. I led the chant.

"I believe—" I shouted loudly.

My teammates yelled back. "I believe!"

"I believe that—" I yelled.

"I believe that!" the Griffons responded.

"I believe that we—" I smiled, knowing the fun part was coming up.

"I believe that we!" the Griffons echoed.

Then we all went nuts, jumping up and down as a group while we moved around in our circle to the right.

"I believe that we will win! I believe that we will win! I believe that we will win! I believe that we will win!" we roared.

"Switch left!" yelled Mirabelle. "I'm getting dizzy!"

We began jumping to the left, chanting "I believe that we will win!" as we went. Then we stopped, extended our arms to the middle of the circle, and piled our hands on top of one another.

CHAPTER TWO

"Yum!" I said as I wrapped my hands around the turkey burger my dad had made for dinner that night. Even when we'd lived in Connecticut, both my parents, especially my mom, had always been strict about what we could eat. Everything had to be healthy, which wasn't always that bad. In fact, like tonight, sometimes it was downright delicious. My dad did most of the cooking. When we moved to California, he started trying some new recipes. Dad's California burger had muenster cheese, lettuce, tomato, and a special ingredient that Dad had invented.

"Extra top secret guac sauce, right?" I asked him before I took my first bite. I loved that stuff.

He smiled. "Of course! I always give you extra top secret guacamole sauce, Devin."

My eight-year-old sister, Maisie, lifted her hamburger bun and peeked under it suspiciously.

"Don't worry, sweetie," he said to her. "Yours is just a burger and cheese, nothing else on it."

Maisie was a picky eater. If my parents would let her, she'd live on only potato chips, cookies, and juice boxes. My mom kept a hidden stash of those items in the house. They came in handy as bribes when my little sister was acting up. Although, lately she'd been in a pretty great mood. It had even been kind of fun to be around her. But I would never have admitted that to her!

The reason she'd been so happy was that she, like me, had been bitten by the soccer bug. We actually had something in common for a change!

"How was practice, girls?" my mom asked as she passed the bowl of sweet potato fries to Maisie, who tried to pass them right over to me. Mom put a couple on her plate anyway and ignored the pout that followed.

"Awesome!" I said, but since my mouth was full of turkey burger, the word came out more like "Agggslurp." I chewed and swallowed. "Sorry. It was awesome!"

"Has Coach Darby eased up at all?" Dad asked.

I nodded. "She's still tough, but she has definitely toned it down a bit. She even smiled for, like, two whole seconds today!"

My parents laughed. "She's the total opposite of Coach Flores, isn't she?" Mom asked.

Coach Flores was the coach of the Kicks. At first

Coach Flores had been so laid back that the Kicks hadn't been able to win a single game. Coach Flores would give everyone a hug for trying and call it a day. But after she saw how much the team wanted to compete, she changed. Now I thought she was the perfect coach—fun-loving, encouraging, and tough when she needed to be.

"They've got completely different coaching styles," I said. "But Coach Darby has been a lot more supportive lately."

"Well, I've got the best coaches ever!" Maisie announced loudly. "Dad, Emma, and Frida. Practice is so much fun. I wish we had it every day!"

Emma and Frida, along with Jessi and Zoe, were my best friends in California. We all played together on the Kicks. Unfortunately, Emma had tried out for the winter league but hadn't made a team. Frida had been away, filming a TV movie (yes, I had a friend who was going to be a movie star!), so she hadn't been able to try out. But the movie had wrapped, and now Emma and Frida were helping my dad coach the elementary school kids.

"Maisie is fast like you, Devin," my dad said. "I think we've got another striker on our hands."

Maisie sat up straight in her chair with a huge grin on her face. She looked very proud of herself.

"Nice, Maisie," I told her. "Wanna kick the ball around after dinner?"

"Yeah!" Maisie said eagerly. "Frida gave me some pointers today. I'll fill you in."

I saw my mom and dad exchange glances as they tried to hide their smiles. One thing Maisie was already a pro at was confidence!

After dinner Maisie and I went out back to practice some drills. I set up cones for us to practice dribbling through. It took no time at all for me to see how Frida had rubbed off on Maisie.

"Okay, so let's pretend that we live near a volcano, Mount Hotsuti," Maisie said, one foot balanced on the ball and her hands on her hips. "We have to zigzag through the cone course as fast as we can to try to make the angry volcano spirits happy. If we do it fast enough, they won't let the volcano erupt."

Frida was an actor who needed to pretend to be someone else on the field. It helped her to focus, and it let her practice acting, too. It really worked for her, and I could see that it worked for Maisie, too. She zoomed through the course as though her life depended on it. I guess in her imagination, it did!

I laughed as I told Kara, my best friend from Connecticut, about it while we video chatted before bed. Well, before her bedtime, anyway. There was a three-hour time difference between Connecticut and California.

"Sounds like Maisie takes after her big sister!" Kara said.

I rolled my eyes. "Maybe she will in soccer. But otherwise we're nothing alike."

Then Kara moved in closer to the screen, squinting at

me. "Hey, I love your hair!" Kara said. "Come closer to the camera."

I leaned in toward my laptop camera so Kara could get a better look.

"Devin!" She sounded shocked. "Do you have highlights?"

I smiled as I tossed my light brown hair over my shoulder. I hadn't been sure if the natural sun streaks were noticeable, so I was really happy that Kara had said something about them.

I nodded. "From the best salon in California—the sun!"

"That's from being out in the sun?" Kara asked in disbelief.

"Yep! Just being outside and playing soccer," I said. "Of course, we all wear sunscreen. But not on our hair!"

"And I love the way you've been wearing it in those beachy waves," Kara complimented me. After my nightly showers I'd been braiding my hair while it was still wet. In the morning I unbraided it, and it was nice and wavy. "You look like such a California surfer girl!"

Kara's compliments made me feel great. When I had first moved to Southern California, I'd been so worried about making friends and fitting in. Not only did I now have friends, but this place was starting to feel like home. And, according to Kara, I even looked like I belonged.

"Well, you look like a total New England girl," I said. Kara was wearing a knit cap and a scarf over her sweater.

"It is so cold here!" Kara shivered. "More snow

tomorrow. The chance of me getting highlights from the sun is zero, which is what the temperature is!

"But seriously," Kara continued, "I am so glad that everything is going so great for you on the Griffons. Things really turned around."

I smiled. "I know. Everything is sooooo much better! And today we came up with our team cheer too. I'm totally stoked to use it at our next game."

"Wait. Did you just say 'stoked'?" Kara asked, crinkling her nose in confusion.

I paused. "Oh yeah!" I said. "You know, *stoked*. Like, I'm excited."

Kara snorted. "I know what it means, Devin!" she said. "But I'm pretty sure that's the most California thing you've ever said."

I shrugged. "I guess I just picked it up, living out here!"

"Wow, Devin." Kara smiled. "You really are a California girl now."

"I guess I am," I replied, liking the sound of that—and that was when the room began to shake.

At first I thought Maisie was bumping around in her room and making the walls vibrate, but then it felt as though the entire house were rocking slowly back and forth. The bottle of water on my desk fell over.

"Devin, what's wrong?" Kara asked, but it felt like her voice was a million miles away.

I jumped up to clean up the water, and I could feel the

floor underneath my feet swaying. My heart was pounding like crazy as I realized what was happening.

"Earthquake!" my dad yelled from downstairs. "Girls, get to your safe spots!"

CHAPTER THREE

Safe spots. Our family had done an earthquake drill a week after we'd moved in, and Mom and Dad had told us where to go if an earthquake happened. For a second my mind was a blank, and then the drill came back to me.

I moved away from the windows and ran to an inside corner of my room, on the wall I shared with Maisie's room. I crouched down and covered my face and head with my arms.

I sat there, frozen in place. Then one of my soccer trophies from Connecticut launched off my bookshelf and almost hit me in the head! It landed with a thud next to me.

I heard footsteps coming up the stairs and my Mom's voice calling out my name. "Devin? Maisie? Are you girls okay?"

I was too afraid to move or even answer her. I thought

the house was still shaking, until I realized it was me that was trembling from head to toe.

I took a deep breath to try to calm my nerves. I put a hand out and touched the wall. It was still. How could my entire house be moving one second and not the next?

Dad ran into my room and bent down to hug me.

"It's okay, Devin. It's over," he said.

I slowly stood up. "So that was an earthquake?"

Dad nodded. "I don't think it was a major one, though."

Mom and Maisie came into my room.

"I got into my safe spot right away," Maisie said proudly.

"I did too, but now I'm wondering how safe it was," I said, and I pointed to the trophy on the floor. "That almost hit me on the head!"

Mom frowned. "I guess we have some more thinking to do about earthquakes," she said.

"You're right," Dad agreed. "I need to go check the rest of the house. Are you sure you girls are okay?"

Maisie and I nodded.

"I actually have a test I'm supposed to be studying for," I realized.

Mom kissed me on the forehead. "Okay, sweetie. I'm glad you're okay."

Mom, Dad, and Maisie left. I picked up the trophy, cleaned up the spilled bottle of water, and sat down at my desk. My laptop lid had shut during the earthquake.

When I opened it, I found Kara anxiously waiting for me.

"Devin, was that really an earthquake?" she asked.

"Yeah," I said. "That was totally weird. I think I'm still shaking."

"Oh my gosh! So everyone's okay? The house didn't break or anything?" she asked.

I started to giggle nervously. "How does a house break?"

"You know what I mean!" Kara said, laughing with me. "Well, I'm so glad you're okay. I can't imagine what that must be like. It sounded pretty crazy over there!"

It had felt pretty crazy too. In fact, I was feeling a little too jarred to keep casually chatting with Kara. Assuring her I was all right, I signed off and then sat down to study for my World Civ test the next day.

We were learning about the Roman empire. Apparently the ancient Romans had had these big arenas where they used to watch gladiators fight each other and even battle it out with wild animals, like lions. And that had been their idea of fun! If you asked me, arenas without soccer were nothing much to brag about. I tried to focus, looking over my notes, where I had jokingly listed "no soccer" as one of the reasons for the decline of the Roman empire.

I flipped the pages of my textbook, trying to find the real answers, but my eyes couldn't settle on what I was trying to read. I noticed that my hand was shaking like crazy as it rested on the page. I tried to ignore it and keep looking, but after a few minutes of staring at the page and not registering anything, I closed the book, sighing. I would just have to wing it. There was no point in studying,

I knew. I couldn't seem to quiet my mind. After all, I'd just experienced my first *earthquake*. How could you act like things were normal when your whole world had literally just shaken beneath you?

If this was what it really meant to be a "California girl," I would be content moving back to Connecticut tomorrow!

CHAPTER FOUR

Jessi was the first friend I saw in the hallway the next morning.

"So, some earthquake last night," I said. "Were you guys okay?"

Jessi shrugged. "Yeah, it was a small one. No big deal."

"Really?" I was surprised. "I don't know. It kind of felt like a big deal to me."

"Oh, wait, was that your first earthquake?" she asked, and I nodded. "Yeah, so I guess it was a big deal for you. Don't worry. You'll get used to it."

"I hope so," I said, but honestly I wasn't sure. Having the house shake under my feet was not something I thought I could ever get used to.

I noticed that some other kids in the hallway were talking about the earthquake too, and I realized I was interested in hearing what they had to say. Almost everyone sounded like Jessi.

"It was a small one."

"No big deal."

And then lunchtime came around, and I was still feeling like the earthquake was a big deal.

I jabbed my fork into the grilled chicken salad my mom had packed for me. Jessi, Zoe, Emma, and Frida were all talking about soccer. Normally I would have joined in, but all I could think about was how scared I'd felt when my house had been shaking.

"So, you guys are playing the Gophers on Saturday, Devin?" Zoe asked.

When I heard my name, it brought me back to attention. I dropped my fork and forced a smile at Zoe.

"Yeah," I said.

"I heard they haven't won a game yet," said Jessi.

"Aw, those poor little Gophers," Emma said. "I remember how it felt when the Kicks never won a game. I hope they win one soon."

"Well, I hope they don't!" Jessi said. "At least not this Saturday, anyway."

Zoe looked at me. "Hey, Devin, you're really quiet. You okay?"

"I guess I'm still upset about that earthquake yesterday," I admitted.

Jessi put her arm around me. "It was her first earthquake!"

"Was there an earthquake last night?" Frida asked, surprised. "I didn't notice it."

Emma nodded. "There was a small one. I think on the news they said it was a 3.9, so that's practically nothing."

Nothing? I felt the color drain from my face. If that was nothing, what would a stronger earthquake be like? I didn't want to find out.

"My mom made me and my dad go outside afterward in case of aftershocks," Jessi said. "So I was happy about it. It was a nice break from homework, and my dad and I got the soccer ball out and started playing."

"Wait, my dad didn't make us go outside," I said. "What are aftershocks? Is that, like, when there's another earthquake after the first one?"

"Yeah," Jessi replied. "But I didn't feel anything yesterday."

I was starting to feel panicky. Why hadn't Dad brought us outside? I tried to remember our earthquake training session. Had he said anything about aftershocks?

Then Emma changed the subject. "So I heard the Spartans won their last game," she said, talking about one of the teams in the boys' winter soccer league.

Frida looked at Jessi. "And I heard that *Cody* scored the game-winning goal," she said.

"With an assist by Steven," Jessi said, grinning at me.

Cody and Steven were friends of ours, and there was some crushing going on between me and Steven and between Cody and Jessi. My parents wouldn't let me go out on dates (and neither would Jessi's), but we were allowed to hang out at the mall and places like that.

And of course, we got to see them in school. Steven and I had World Civ and English together. Most days we got a chance to talk when we walked from one class to the other. A lot of our conversations were about soccer, because Steven was a fanatic like me.

"We really should go out and see one of their games," Zoe suggested. "But with the winter league schedule, it's hard to find the time."

"Steven mentioned that he and Cody were going to try to come to the Griffons game this Saturday," I said, and Jessi got a big smile on her face. "The Spartans are playing in the afternoon. I think it's one of the first times our game schedules don't conflict."

"If Cody is in the stands, I'll have to show him how it's done," Jessi said, her eyes gleaming. "Look for me to score a flawless hat trick at Saturday's game."

"I would love to score a hat trick in a game," said Zoe. "Do you really think you could?"

"If Coach keeps me in for more than a quarter, I bet I could," Jessi said.

"Well, I hope you do," I said. "I want to win this game! I think the Griffons have a good shot at being the winter league champions."

"Wait a second," Zoe said. "The Gators are a strong team. We've got our eye on the championship too."

That was the weirdest thing about the winter

league—that the Kicks didn't get to stay together on the same team. Zoe and the Kicks former co-captain, Grace, played for the Gators, and I knew we were going to have to face them later in the season. I had thought about what it would be like to have Zoe on the opposing team, and to maybe even try to steal the ball from her. Like I said—weird!

"You guys have a great record so far," I said, and then suddenly a loud boom filled the air. The floor under my feet began vibrating, and I felt a wave of panic wash over me. It was another earthquake!

I almost dove under the table, before I saw out of the corner of my eye one of the school's custodians. He had been folding up one of the large lunch tables, and had dropped it. It had hit the floor and caused the loud bang and shaking I had felt.

"Devin?" I barely heard Jessi over the sound of the blood pumping through my ears.

"Um, what?" I asked, totally flustered.

"Are you okay?" she asked. "I don't think you heard a word I said."

"Yeah. No, I'm good," I lied. I knew I could tell me friends anything, but thinking a falling table was an earthquake was pretty embarrassing! I didn't want them to think I was losing it.

Just then the bell rang. I grabbed my bag and headed toward the doors, waving at Jessi, Zoe, Emma, and Frida as I darted out.

I noticed that my heart was still beating like crazy as I headed to my class. The earthquake might have been over, but I guess I was still feeling my own emotional after-shocks. Would I ever be able to shake them off?

CHAPTER FIVE

I got to World Civ and slid into my seat just before the bell rang. Steven sat a few seats away from me. I nodded at him, and he smiled. He really had the most awesome smile.

Then the bell rang, and a girl came into the room, looking a little lost. I didn't recognize her. She had curly brown hair and freckles on her cheeks, and her backpack looked heavy, like it held every book for every class.

Mr. Emmet, our teacher, looked up from the folder he was leafing through.

"You must be Hailey," he said, smiling at her, and she gave him a relieved smile back.

"That's me," she said.

Mr. Emmet stood up. "Everyone, this is Hailey Kocek. It's her first day here," he said. Then he turned to Hailey. "You can take that empty seat in the third row. We're having a test today, and you're off the hook for that. While everyone's taking the test, I'll get you up to speed on what we've been learning."

Hailey nodded. "Thanks," she replied, and she took the empty seat, which happened to be right next to Steven. She smiled at him, and I noticed that he smiled right back.

"Okay, guys. Clear your desks. It's test time," Mr. Emmet said, and he began to hand out the tests.

I started to feel sweaty. I wasn't a genius or anything, but I was a good student, and part of the reason was because I always studied. It was just like soccer practice. If I didn't practice soccer, I'd be a bad soccer player. And if I didn't study, I would probably fail a lot of tests.

But I hadn't been able to concentrate on studying after the earthquake had hit. How was I going to pass this test?

Maybe you'll know the answers, I thought hopefully, but as soon as I looked at the first question, I knew I was in trouble.

List three causes of the decline of the Roman empire.

I swear, the only thing that popped into my head was "no soccer," the joke answer I had written in my notes. But of course I couldn't write that down. I racked my brain, trying to remember.

Something about gladiators? I thought, but no, gladiators hadn't caused the decline of the Roman empire, had they?

I started to panic. I felt like I was on the field surrounded by defenders, with no one in sight to pass to. I was out of moves.

I took a few deep breaths and stared at my paper. Mr. Emmet must have noticed that my pen wasn't moving.

"Everything all right, Devin?" he asked, looking up from the book he was showing to Hailey.

"Um, yeah, fine," I lied. What was I going to say? That I hadn't studied because of the earthquake? The earthquake that didn't seem to be a big deal to anybody except me?

So I took another deep breath and started writing. When Mom helped me study, she always encouraged me to look for the questions that I knew the answers to and start with them. So I filled in a few answers that I was pretty sure I got right. For the rest I made my best guess (another Mom strategy). But would it be enough to pass the test? I wasn't sure.

And that would lead to another problem. In order to play on a soccer team, I had to get good grades. That was the rule of the school league, but Mom and Dad had always made it clear that it was their rule too, even though they knew I was a good student. How would I explain this failed test to them? How would an F affect my World Civ grade?

I looked at the clock and then frantically started trying to fill in the answers I had skipped. But I had only filled in a few when Mr. Emmet called out to the class.

"Time's up. Please pass up your papers," he said, and I sighed and put down my pen. As he collected the papers, I mentally tried to figure out my current class grade based on the work I'd done so far. If I failed this test, would I fail the class? But I'd gotten an 85 on my first project, and a 93 on the last quiz. . . .

Then the bell rang. I was looking forward to walking to English class with Steven. I knew he would probably say something funny or nice that would help me forget all about failing the test and freaking out about the earthquake.

But when I got up from my desk, Steven was not in his seat, waiting for me like he usually did. He and Hailey were walking out the door together!

I guess I could have caught up to them and introduced myself to Hailey. That was probably what I should have done. But instead I just stood there, confused.

Why was Steven walking with Hailey and not me? We *always* walked together. Always. This change made me feel strange.

I walked by myself to English class, and Steven noticed me as he took his seat.

"Oh, hey, Devin," he said. "Have you met Hailey yet?"

"Yeah. I mean, not really. You know, just in our last class," I said, not making any sense at all.

"Nice to meet you," Hailey said in a perfectly nice way, but I was feeling flustered and awkward, and I quickly took my seat.

Jessi sat next to me in English. She had been chatting with Cody but stopped when I sat down, and she leaned over to me. "What's up, Devin?" she said with a look of concern on her face. I guessed she could tell just by looking at me that something was wrong.

I was starting to whisper into her ear, when our English teacher said loudly, "Quiet! Books out. Turn to page ninety-six."

I shrugged and mouthed "Talk to you later" as class began. Luckily, I didn't have an English test to fail. But I was still rattled when the final bell rang, and we had to hustle to get to practice since it was now at Pinewood. I didn't have a chance to talk with Jessi until we were dressed and warming up on the field.

"So what do you think?" I asked after I had told her the whole story about Hailey.

"Well, he's probably just being nice because she's new," Jessi said. "That's why you like him, right? Because he's nice?" She bent her right knee and started doing lunges.

"Yeah, you're right," I said, but it still didn't feel right. To be honest, nothing felt right. Between the earthquake, and failing the test, and Steven not walking with me to English, I was feeling pretty shaken up!

Then Coach blew her whistle, and we jogged out onto the field. I liked the feel of my feet pounding on the neatly trimmed grass. I fell into a rhythm as Coach had the team do some laps.

At least there's one place where I don't feel shaky, I thought. *The soccer field!*

CHAPTER SIX

On Saturday morning I jumped out of bed as soon as my alarm clock went off at seven a.m. On a school morning I'd have hit the snooze button and rolled over. But today was a game day, and every game day felt like Christmas morning. I had to admit, I hadn't felt that way when I'd first joined the Griffons. But now that we were acting more like a team, I loved going to games again.

I hurried to get dressed in my pink, white, and blue Griffons uniform. I didn't like it as much as my Kicks uniform, but it did have a cool emblem of a griffon on the front. A griffon was a mythical beast that was half lion, half eagle, which I thought was a pretty cool mascot for a soccer team. It was a combination of two swift and deadly predators.

Maybe that's why most of the Griffons are so ruthless on the field, I mused as I pulled my hair into a ponytail. Some of our players were so aggressive during games that it was a wonder we didn't get more penalties. The Kicks weren't like that at all. Our mascot was a kangaroo, a cute, friendly animal that hopped around—but a kangaroo was also an amazingly strong kicker. Both teams were equally strong, I thought. But the style of play was really different on each team, and I thought I liked the Kicks style better.

I ran downstairs, where Mom had breakfast ready for me. We'd been trying out new carb-protein combinations before a game to see what gave me the most energy. This morning she'd made me a bowl of her homemade granola with low-fat milk and fresh blueberries, and two hard-boiled eggs.

"I'm eating the same breakfast as you," Maisie announced as I sat down at the table. "I have a big practice today."

"But you hate hard-boiled eggs!" I said.

Maisie took a big bite out of one of her eggs. "Not any-more." She started to make a face, but then she gulped it down without complaining.

Then I realized something. "Maisie has a practice? Does that mean you won't be at the game?" I asked Dad. He'd never missed any of my games. Once, he had a bad cold, but he came anyway, and I could hear him sneezing all the way out on the field!

"Of course I'll be at your game," Dad said. "I scheduled Maisie's practice for later this afternoon."

After breakfast Mom, Dad, Maisie, and I left for the

Pinewood Rec Center. Pinewood was a nearby town that was a lot fancier than Kentville, which meant it had a super nice soccer field. When the school league started up and I was playing with the Kicks again, the nice soccer field would probably be the thing I missed most about being on the Griffons. The Kicks' field was decent, but not as fancy as Pinewood's.

We got to the field at eight fifteen sharp. The game started at nine, so Mom, Dad, and Maisie went to stake out the best spot in the bleachers, while I went to warm up with the team.

There were eighteen players on the Griffons, and eleven at a time were on the field during a game. When I'd first joined the Griffons, the only players I'd known had been Jessi, Zarine, and Sarah, all from the Kicks; Mirabelle, who'd been on the Kicks briefly, before transferring to Pinewood; and Jamie, who had tried to sabotage the Kicks.

It hadn't been easy getting to know the other twelve members of the team—not because they'd been unfriendly (although a few of them had been, to begin with) but because Coach Darby hadn't done a lot of teamwork exercises with us. That had changed a little bit once she'd seen that we played better once we had learned how to communicate with one another.

"Devin, ready?" Coach called out to me.

"Ready!" I called back, and then I launched into our pregame ritual—which I had taught the team.

I did a cartwheel. "Lauren!" I cried, naming one of my teammates.

Lauren did a cartwheel. "Katie!" she called out.

Every player took a turn until every girl had been called on. By the time the last girl had done her cartwheel, our energy was pumped up for the game. We got even more pumped up by getting together in a circle and doing the "I Believe" chant together.

"All right, girls. Let's do some passing drills to warm up!" Coach shouted, and everyone hurried to line up.

Before the drills started, I looked up into the stands. There were Dad, Mom, and Maisie. I checked to see if Steven and Cody were there, like they had said they would be, but I didn't see them anywhere. That bugged me a little bit. On Thursday and Friday, Steven had walked with Hailey to English class again, and I hadn't had a chance to remind him about the game.

"Devin, look alive!" Coach called out, and that was when I noticed the ball whizzing past my feet. The drill had started, but I hadn't been paying attention.

"Sorry, Coach!" I called out, and chased after the ball.

It wasn't the best way to start things off. I tried to really focus for the rest of the warm-up, to get my head in the game. The Griffons had just started winning, and we couldn't afford to lose if we were going to win the championship!

When warm-up was over, Coach Darby called out the starting lineup. I was psyched that she put me in midfield with Jessi and Sasha. I hadn't had a strong start to the winter season, but I had worked hard to prove to Coach Darby that I was a good player. The fact that she was starting me showed that she believed in me.

So I was feeling pretty good when I got out onto the field. The Gophers got control of the ball first. Jessi swiped the ball from the Gophers' forward as the girl was dribbling down the field. Then Jessi passed it to me.

I dribbled toward the Gophers' goal. From the corner of my eye, I could see one of the Gophers coming for me. I needed to pass, and Jamie was open. I slowed down, and then I kicked.

As I connected with the ball, I felt my foot slip. Instead of shooting straight to Jamie, the ball veered sharply to the right—and directly in front of the feet of one of the Gophers!

Jamie scowled and chased after the ball. I looked down. What had happened? And then I noticed that my right shoe was untied.

What an embarrassing pass! And I couldn't just stop and fix my shoe, so I ran around with my lace flapping until the next time-out was called.

"Nice pass back there, Devin," Jamie said, walking past me. "You know you're on the *Griffons*, right?"

I cringed inside but didn't answer her. That had been a horrible attempt at a pass. Yes, it had been an accident, but I felt like I deserved her comment.

I didn't do anything else embarrassing for the rest of

the quarter, thank goodness—but I didn't score any goals either. So I wasn't surprised that Coach Darby benched me when the quarter was up—although, thanks to goals by Jamie and Sasha, the Griffons were up, 2–0.

Jessi flashed me a sympathetic look as I jogged off the field and Tracey ran in to replace me.

I watched the second quarter from the bench. The Gophers were having a rough game. Jessi, Jamie, and Tracey each scored—and the Gophers couldn't manage a single goal.

At halftime Tracey ran back to the bench, her dark eyes shining.

"I scored a goal! Finally!" she said. "This must be my lucky game."

Jessi was grinning too. "I'm one third of the way to my hat trick," she boasted. Then she looked up at the stands. "Even though it doesn't look like Cody's here to see it."

"Yeah," I said. "Although, I'm kind of glad Steven wasn't here to see me make that pass."

I was itching to get back into the game, to prove to Coach that I was a better player than that pass. But I didn't get my way. She kept me on the bench for the rest of the game.

Jessi got to play one more quarter. She made a second goal, but she didn't get her hat trick. The Gophers managed to score twice, but that wasn't enough to save them. The Griffons won, 7–2.

When the game was over, I stood up, pasted a smile

onto my face, and cheered with the rest of my team. But I didn't jump up and down or hug anybody. I just didn't want to, which was not like me at all. Normally I'd have been really happy for my team, no matter what.

What is wrong with me? I wondered.

"Devin, what's bugging you?" Jessi asked me.

"Being benched," I replied, but that wasn't all of it. Something was wrong, and I could feel it.

Was I losing my soccer mojo?

CHAPTER SEVEN

"Well, cheer up," Jessi said as we walked back to the stands. "In a little while you'll be eating pizza and laughing when Emma accidentally gives herself another tomato sauce mustache."

"That's right. I'd forgotten about our pizza date," I replied. Last night my four friends and I had all texted and checked our schedules and decided that we could meet for a Saturday lunch. Anytime I got a chance to be with Jessi, Emma, Zoe, and Frida all in one place was a good time. I hoped our get-together would be the pick-me-up I needed.

"Devin, you hardly played!" Maisie cried out loudly as she ran toward me, followed by our parents.

"Ugh, *Maisie!*" I snapped, and then Maisie got that sad look she got when her feelings were hurt.

I sighed. "Sorry. I just didn't need the news blast about how I got benched."

"Everyone has a bad game from time to time," Dad said. "The important thing is that you tried your best."

"I tried my best, but my shoelace came untied," I said. "It's so unfair!"

"Life isn't always going to be fair," Mom said. "You just have to make the best of it."

"I guess so," I replied. "Mom, after we get home, can you give me a ride to Pizza Kitchen? I'm meeting my friends there at noon."

"Oh, honey, you should have checked with me," Mom said. "I made appointments for you and Maisie at the dentist at noon."

I groaned. "Do I have to?"

"Devin, you haven't had your teeth checked since we moved to California," Mom said. "I would be a terrible parent if I canceled this appointment."

"No, you'd be a great parent for letting your daughter spend some much needed social time with her friends," I said, hoping desperately to change her mind. But she was not moved.

"Sorry, Devin," Mom said firmly, and I knew there was no point in arguing.

Talk about not fair! Instead of having pizza with my friends I was stuck going to the dentist.

I turned to Jessi. "Tell everyone I'm sorry," I said. I

couldn't bear to text them myself. I was too bummed out.

I was silent for the ride home, but it didn't matter, because Maisie kept talking and talking about her team's first game tomorrow. After we got home, I showered and got dressed for the dentist, and I made sure to bring my earbuds with me to the car so I wouldn't have to listen to Maisie the whole way.

To be honest, I was pretty nervous about going to the dentist. Back in Connecticut I'd had the same dentist for as long I could remember, Dr. Benson. He was an okay dentist. His walls were painted the color of pea soup, and the music he played didn't have anybody singing along. Going to the dentist was never fun, but at least I'd always known what to expect.

I had no idea what this new dentist would be like—and I wasn't sure I wanted to find out.

Mom finally pulled up in front of a little brick building painted yellow. It looked cheerful, I thought. Once we got inside, the walls were painted pale blue, and there were rainbows on them. I looked around and saw a colorful set of blocks and some plastic trucks, and then I realized I was the only kid in the waiting room older than ten.

"Mom, is this a little kids' dentist?" I hissed as we sat down on a blue couch to wait.

"Dr. Sonya is a pediatric dentist, yes," Mom replied.

"So a dentist for little kids," I repeated. "But I'm not a little kid!"

Mom sighed. "No, you're not, but you're not an adult yet either," she said. "I'm sure Dr. Sonya has lots of other patients your age."

The receptionist looked up from the desk. "Ms. Burke, which of your daughters would like to go first?" she asked.

"Maisie!" I said.

"Me!" Maisie cried out at the same time. Of course. Only someone like Maisie would be excited about going to the dentist.

"I'll stay with Maisie," Mom said. "It'll be your turn soon."

Twenty minutes later a young guy in a white coat came into the waiting room.

"Devin? I'm Marc. I'll be cleaning your teeth today," he said.

"Okay. Um, thanks," I said, and Marc ushered me into a room with one of those big chairs with the little sink attached.

Marc cleaned my teeth with one of those scrapey things, and then polished them, and it didn't hurt as bad as I remembered. When he finally finished, he tried to hand me a sticker of a smiling puppy that said, MY TEETH ARE CLEAN! but that was just too much.

"No, thanks," I said, and Marc shrugged.

Then he led me to another room, where Maisie was sitting on a regular chair with Mom and wearing a sticker with a smiling duck on it that read, NO CAVITIES!

"This must be Devin," said a woman in a light blue doctor's coat. She had a friendly smile and wore her long, dark brown hair in a single side braid. "I'm Dr. Sonya. Have a seat."

"Hi," I said.

"Devin, do you want Maisie and me to stay?" Mom asked.

"No. I think I got this," I replied, trying to sound as mature as possible.

"I got no cavities, Devin! Bet you can't beat me!" Maisie challenged me as Mom walked her out.

"It's not a contest, Maisie," I said wearily.

"I'm sure you'll do just fine, Devin," Dr. Sonya assured me.

I settled into the dentist chair, a dental assistant named Kathy came in, and Dr. Sonya began to poke around in my mouth. It was slightly less annoying than when Marc had been scraping my teeth, because Dr. Sonya was a lot gentler.

"Okay, Devin," she said after a few minutes. "I see you have three cavities."

"Three?" I asked, horrified.

"Do you floss your teeth every day?" she asked.

I had to think about that. I pretty much flossed only when Mom said, "Devin! Don't forget to floss your teeth tonight!"

"Um, not really," I admitted.

"So, you might want to start flossing regularly," she said. "In the meantime we'll get you an appointment to have those three cavities taken care of."

I nodded. "Okay. Thanks."

Kathy brought me back to the waiting room, and Mom went to the counter to get our paperwork. I saw her eyes go wide when she saw that I needed another appointment.

She actually turned around and said, "Three cavities, Devin?"

I shrugged.

"I win! I win!" Maisie cried triumphantly.

I ignored Maisie. I couldn't wait to get out of there, but Mom was taking forever at the counter.

Finally Mom finished up, and we left the office. Maisie was skipping and singing the whole way back to the car.

"I win! I win! I win!"

"Quiet, Maisie. It wasn't a contest!" I snapped, and I slammed the door when I climbed into the front passenger seat.

"Was so!" Maisie said. "Devin might be better at soccer than me, but I'm better at teeth!"

I looked at my mother. "Mom!" I pleaded.

"Maisie, there was no contest," Mom said. "I am very proud of you for having no cavities. But please don't make Devin feel bad about it."

"Okay," Maisie said as the car pulled out of the parking lot. "Maybe I can help Devin. Dr. Sonya said I should keep doing exactly what I'm doing to keep my teeth clean. I can show you how to brush and floss the right way when we get home, if you want."

Thanks to messing up in the game and being benched and missing lunch with my friends, I was in a terrible mood. So when Maisie said that, I was sure she was trying to rub in the fact that I had three cavities and she didn't.

I exploded. "MOM! Make her stop."

"Now, Devin, Maisie's just trying to be nice," Mom said.

"She is NOT trying to be nice," I said. "How can you not see that? She's trying to bug me on purpose."

"I am not! I'm trying to help!" Maisie protested. But I swore I detected a defiant little twinkle in her eyes. I wasn't buying the innocent act.

"Devin, lower your voice, please," Mom said.

"Yes, lower your voice," Maisie added.

"See what I mean?" I asked Mom.

"I'm just trying to be nice because you lost the cavity contest and I won," Maisie said.

"It was NOT a contest!" I insisted.

"Was so, because I said so," Maisie said.

I turned to look at the backseat. "SHUT UP ALREADY!"

"Devin!" Mom scolded. She looked at me, shocked. "We do not say 'shut up' in this family! You know that! Now calm down, young lady."

"You need to tell Maisie to calm down," I argued.

"You are both behaving badly," Mom said. "Maisie, no television for you this weekend."

Maisie pouted, and I felt pretty happy about that—until Mom dropped the next piece of news.

"And, Devin, no phone or video chatting this weekend," Mom added.

"WHAT?" I shrieked. "But I need to video chat with Kara. She'll wonder what's wrong."

"You may text her right now and explain that you can't chat with her tonight," Mom said. "Then you will give me your phone when we get home."

Things could not be any worse, I thought as I took out my phone to text Kara. Then I noticed a text from Coach Darby.

Our game with the Grizzlies has been moved to tomorrow. 2 p.m. in Rancho Verdes.

"We have a game tomorrow," I announced.

"No fair!" Maisie wailed. "I have a game tomorrow. We can't both have a game!"

"We'll figure it out when we get all the details," Mom said with a sigh. "Honestly, can't you two girls stop arguing just for five minutes?"

I put my earbuds in and listened to music on my phone for the rest of the ride. Obviously things *could* get worse, and they already had—because Dad coached Maisie's team, and he couldn't be in two places at once. And Mom wouldn't want to miss Maisie's first game either. Which would mean no cheering section in the stands for me.

I knew we were close to home, so I sent my text to Kara.

Can't video chat this weekend because of a stupid fight with Maisie. Everything is awful.

Kara replied quickly.

☹

Yep, that frowny face summed things up exactly.

CHAPTER EIGHT

I could barely eat my dinner that night, I was so upset about the absolutely awful day I'd had. It didn't help that Maisie was bragging to my dad about her awesome dental checkup. But I let her talk, because I didn't want to get into any more trouble! It was time for things to get better, not worse.

When dinner was over, Maisie went up to her room, but my parents asked me to stick around so they could talk to me.

"Devin, we don't want you to worry about us not coming to tomorrow's game," my mom said in a gentle tone. It didn't help. I was still mad at her for not realizing that the fight about the dentist was all Maisie's fault. "Maisie's game is at one, and yours is at two. We can do both."

"But they're so close together," I pointed out.

"Maisie's game won't be as long as a middle school game," Dad said. "We might miss the first few minutes of your game, but we will be there. I promise. I haven't missed one of your games yet, and I'm not about to start now!" He smiled. "Okay?"

I nodded. "Okay," I said flatly, not believing they could possibly make it in time. "Can I be excused now?"

My mom and dad exchanged glances before my mom answered, "Of course."

I headed up to my room to *not* video chat with Kara and to *not* text with Jessi, Frida, Emma, and Zoe. I figured I would go stare at the wall until I fell asleep. But the problem was, I couldn't fall asleep. I kept staring at the trophy on my shelf, remembering how it had almost fallen onto my head. And when I did fall asleep, I tossed and turned all night.

The next morning I had dark circles under my eyes. Great! I felt like I hadn't slept at all. It was definitely not the way I wanted to start a game day.

My mom had arranged for me to ride to the game with Jessi and her parents, since both of my parents would be at Maisie's game. It felt weird. I was so used to my pre-game ritual of riding in the Marshmallow (that was what my family called our white minivan) with my ear buds in, listening to music to get me pumped up. Not that Jessi's parents weren't super nice, because they were, and

I always liked hanging out with Jessi. But it just didn't feel right.

"Why didn't you answer any of my texts last night?" Jessi whispered to me in the backseat.

I sighed. "Because Maisie is clearly on this planet to ruin my life," I said, before I launched into the sad tale of the kiddie dentist.

Jessi, who didn't have any brothers or sisters, shook her head in sympathy. "That stinks, Devin. Sometimes I wish I had a little sister, but not when I hear stories like that. Anyway, cheer up! Today is game day, the day you live for!"

I hadn't jumped out of bed this morning like it was Christmas. Instead I had dragged myself out, wondering what new disaster would happen today.

I forced a smile for Jessi's sake. "Yeah!" I tried to sound peppy, but I couldn't convince myself—or Jessi.

"You'll feel better once you're on the field," Jessi said so confidently that I almost believed her.

But things did not get better right away. When we did our pregame cartwheels, I fell over and ate grass. I half-heartedly chanted along with the rest of the team for "I Believe," and during warm-ups I felt stiff and clunky.

We were playing on the soccer field at Rancho Verdes Middle School. The field didn't have bleachers, so people coming to the games had to bring their own chairs. It looked like a party, with a lot of the parents bringing coolers full of food and sitting under umbrellas.

My face must have fallen when I didn't spot my parents with the other families. Jessi noticed. "What's wrong?" she asked.

"It's just so weird not seeing my parents in the crowd," I said. "I'm used to them cheering me on. I don't see how they are going to make it to my game and to Maisie's, too."

Jamie, who had been warming up next to us, looked at me. "Sorry, but you better get used to it," she said. "It'll be easier if you do." But she didn't say it in her usual bratty way. In fact, she almost sounded sympathetic. I looked at her for a second, unsure what to make of her comment. I was about to ask her what she meant, when Coach called us all together.

"We're facing the Grizzlies today. They're undefeated. We're going to need to put in our best effort," said Coach Darby in her no-nonsense way. "Devin, Kelly, and Mirabelle, you're starting as forwards. Get out there and get aggressive right away. We need to set the tone for this game from the start and force the Grizzlies to chase after that ball. We can't give them an inch."

I felt a momentary surge of happiness. If Coach thought we needed to put our best foot forward and she'd chosen to start me, maybe it meant she *did* believe in me, even after that bad pass yesterday. I was determined to prove to Coach Darby that she could trust me.

That was probably why I was way too overeager when I hit the field. The Griffons' midfielders got possession of the ball immediately, and Kristin passed it to me. I shot forward to meet it and ran a little ahead of it to get as close to the goal as possible. I aimed and sent a perfect kick into the goal, just out of reach of the goalie's outstretched arms.

The referee's whistle blew. "Offsides!" he shouted.

I was so excited at the idea of scoring during the first few seconds of the game that I hadn't realized that I had outrun the Grizzlies' defenders, when I should have backed up to receive Kristin's pass. Since I was offsides, the goal was no good. I heard our team groan in disappointment.

"Pay attention, Devin!" Coach Darby yelled.

And that wasn't my only mistake. I was so shaken up that I missed an easy pass, and a Grizzlies defender came in and stole the ball. One of their forwards took it down the field and scored. Griffons 0, Grizzlies 1.

I felt like the goal was totally my fault! Again I checked the spectators, hoping to see my parents' faces to give me a surge of support so I could shake off the way I had been playing. But they weren't there, and while I was looking for them, I missed another pass. The second in a matter of minutes! I couldn't believe it. My face turned bright red. I felt totally mortified.

My shoulders slumped as the whistle blew, signaling the end of the first quarter. Coach Darby was waiting for me on the sidelines.

"Devin, I don't know what's going on with you today,

but we can't afford these kinds of mistakes," she said, as blunt as always. "You're out and Jamie is in."

Jamie jogged onto the field without even looking at me. I slumped onto the ground, feeling completely embarrassed at how I had played. This was just like the last game all over again! Only this time it was bad playing. I couldn't blame it on a shoelace.

"You can't win them all, Devin," Katie, benched too, said to me. I guessed she was trying to cheer me up. But it just made me feel even more self-conscious.

"Yeah," I said as I fixed my eyes on the field, pretending to be absorbed in watching the game. Katie took the hint and didn't say anything else, which was a relief. I didn't feel like talking.

The Grizzlies had turned up their aggressiveness and tightened their defense. Jamie had squeezed through their defense and had a clear path to the goal, when a Grizzlies defender slid toward her, looking like she was trying to trip Jamie. Yet at the last minute Jamie was able to deftly turn herself and the ball away, maneuvering around the defender and giving herself a clear shot at the goal. She took it and scored. Griffons 1, Grizzlies 1.

When the Grizzlies saw how dangerous Jamie was, they overcompensated by concentrating on her. It gave Mirabelle some breathing room, and Sasha in midfield sent her a pass that led to another scoring opportunity for the Griffons. We were now 2–1.

I heard a familiar voice cheering from the sidelines. I looked across the field and saw my dad, hooting and hollering about the goal my team had just made. He met my eyes and waved at me enthusiastically. Mom and Maisie, who was still in her soccer uniform, were sitting with him, clapping and cheering too. It felt so good to see them that for a moment I forgot how horrible I had played. Then I remembered and just felt terrible all over again. At least my family hadn't been there to see it.

After Mirabelle scored, the Grizzlies seemed unsure about who to cover. The defenders couldn't control Mirabelle or Jamie, who were consistently breaking free and dribbling through the defense. They were aided by our midfielders and defenders, who were dominating the ball. With that kind of pressure, the Griffons were able to put two more balls into the net.

When the game ended 4–1, my teammates went wild. After all, we had just beaten an undefeated team. Even though I joined the group hug and cheer, I felt totally empty. The win had had nothing to do with me. And yes, soccer was a team sport, but the only thing I had done this game was to help the Grizzlies score their only goal. I didn't deserve to celebrate.

I couldn't get over the fact that my mistake had caused the Grizzlies to score. Yesterday I hadn't helped my team at all. Today I had actually hurt them.

I knew what Dad would say. *Every player has a bad*

CHAPTER NINE

On Sunday night Mom surprised me and Maisie at supper.

"You girls have been behaving nicely since yesterday," she said. "If you can both apologize to each other, I think we can restore your privileges."

Privileges—meaning I could finally video chat with Kara again! Apologizing was not going to be a problem, especially since I wasn't feeling mad at Maisie anymore.

"Maisie, I really am sorry I told you to shut up," I said. "I was having a really bad day, and I didn't mean to hurt your feelings."

"And I'm sorry too," Maisie said.

We both looked expectantly at my mom.

"Fine," she said. "Your privileges are restored."

"Yay! TV!" Maisie cheered, and I hurried to finish my broccoli and brown rice. I couldn't wait to talk with Kara! I hadn't talked to her since Friday night, and I had so much to tell her—my two bad games, and the disastrous dentist trip.

Kara's eyes got wide when I finished my story.

"You are *not* thinking of quitting soccer!" she said. "You can't! It's your life!"

"But what if I'm not meant to play?" I asked. "I mean, just because you love something doesn't mean you're going to be good at it."

"But you *are* good at it," Kara insisted.

I sighed. "I haven't been good at anything since the earthquake."

Kara's blue eyes got so wide, I thought they might pop out of her head. "Devin, maybe you've been cursed by the earthquake!"

I laughed. "Kara, how can an earthquake curse you?"

She shrugged. "I don't know, but it's when all your bad luck started," she said. She ducked her head as she began typing on her keyboard. "You need good luck instead of bad. Let's see if there is something on the Internet that will help."

Her eyes began skimming over her screen, looking at the search results. "This one looks good! Now repeat after me, 'Bad luck, bad luck, you're a schmuck, time to go in the garbage truck. Sun above and land below, time to make the good luck flow!'"

I repeated the words after her, laughing the whole time. "Come on!" I cried. "This can't be real. Somebody just put this on the Internet so people would make fools of themselves."

"Oh wait!" she suddenly cried. "You're doing it wrong. You have to hop three times in a clockwise circle on one foot while you're saying it. Like this!"

Kara stood up and demonstrated. I could see only the middle of her body as she hopped around. She looked ridiculous! Then she looked back into the camera.

"Okay, this may not be real, but it's fun!" she said.

I got up from my desk chair and started hopping on one foot in a circle as Kara read the words of the chant to me again. When I got to the part about making the good luck flow, I accidentally hopped right onto the leg of my computer chair.

"Whoa!" I said as I toppled to the floor.

The chair rolled away and fell onto its side as I heard Kara yelling, "Devin! Devin! Are you okay?"

I staggered up and grinned into the computer camera. "No broken bones. I think I'll live. But I don't think it's a good sign that I had bad luck right in the middle of the good luck chant!"

Kara laughed just as my dad stuck his head into the room. He noticed the desk chair toppled over and looked at me with a raised eyebrow. "Devin, honey, are you all right?"

"Kara and I were just trying to undo my bad luck. It didn't work out so great," I said as I pointed to the chair.

"Hi, Kara!" My dad leaned into the camera and waved. "How are things going?"

They chatted for a few moments while I righted my chair and wheeled it back over to the desk.

"Devin, are you done talking to Kara? Could we talk for a little bit?" he asked. I nodded and said good-bye to Kara.

"You'll see!" Kara told me encouragingly before she signed off. "Nothing but good luck from now on!"

"Let's head outside," said my dad. "It's a nice night."

We went downstairs, and Dad flipped on the backyard light. It was almost fully dark. He jogged up to a soccer ball on the grass and passed it to me.

"So what's this about bad luck?" he asked with a frown on his face. "Is everything okay?"

"Not really," I admitted. "I made that bad pass yesterday, and today you missed it, but I made a really bad play. And it's not just soccer. Everything's been going wrong since the earthquake. I can't sleep, and I think I failed a test, for the first time in my life!"

I started dribbling the ball around the yard. It felt good to be moving instead of sitting around worrying.

"So this all started with the earthquake." Dad stroked his chin thoughtfully. "I wish you had told me or your mother how upset you were about the earthquake. You didn't say anything."

"I guess that's because everyone else was acting like it was no big deal," I said, coming to a stop in front of him. "Even Maisie didn't seem bothered by it, and she's younger than me."

"It's a scary thing. It threw me, too," he said.

"*You* were scared?" I asked incredulously. I couldn't believe it.

He nodded. "Sure. The earth moved! That's not something I'm used to happening. But then I reminded myself of all the safety plans we have in place as a family. That makes me feel better. And I also thought about how common earthquakes are. Minor ones happen thousands of times every day. Major ones are rare."

"They happen thousands of times every day?" I asked in disbelief.

"Yes, and most of the time you can't even feel them," he said. "So would it help if we went over our earthquake readiness plan and did a few more drills as a family?"

I nodded. "Yeah, I would like that, Dad."

Dad smiled. "We'll have a family earthquake night when we can make sure we are totally prepared for another quake. We can even make it into a party."

I smiled. Leave it to my dad to make earthquakes fun!

"You know, Devin," he said, "part of the reason why the earthquake was so scary for me is because I like to be in control. I like planning out our dinners and knowing what I'm going to be doing at work each day and being prepared so I'm ready for it. There is no controlling an earthquake, only our response to it. I think you're a lot like me. From the soccer field to your homework, you're always in control. The earthquake has shaken that up for you. But once you feel balanced again, you'll feel a lot better. What do you think?"

Have I mentioned how much I love my dad? I gave him a hug.

"One last thing, Devin," he said. "I know you were upset

about the soccer game today. I'm sorry I wasn't there for all of it. I hope you know how much it means to me to be at your games. I'll always do everything in my power to be there, cheering you on."

"It just felt weird not having you guys there the entire time," I said. "But after it was all over with, I'm glad you didn't see me play. I was terrible!"

"You'll get them next time, Devin," he encouraged me. "Everyone has a bad game every now and then. Even the most famous soccer players in the world."

I knew Dad was trying to help. But that was the same thing he always told me when I had a bad game, and right now it wasn't making me feel any better.

"It wasn't just one bad game; it was two," I reminded him. "Two in a row."

And I think I've lost my soccer mojo and that maybe I shouldn't even be playing anymore, I wanted to add, but I stopped myself. Kara was right—I *did* love soccer. Maybe this was just a slump.

"Learn from your experience and move on, Devin," Dad told me. "That's all you can do."

I knew Dad meant well, but his lecture was just making me feel sad. So I decided to turn it around.

"That's not *all* I can do," I said, and then I started hopping around in a circle on one foot, and Dad laughed. He started hopping around on one foot with me.

Maisie ran out into the yard. "What are you guys doing?"

"We're getting rid of bad luck!" I told her.

Maisie looked thoughtful. "I don't have any bad luck. Can I do it anyway?"

"Of course!" Dad called out.

Maisie started hopping along with us. "I'm getting dizzy!"

Soon we were all cracking up, and then we had a hopping race across the yard. (Dad won, but I think that was because he had the longest legs.)

Maybe Kara's hopping chant worked, and maybe it didn't. But it definitely made me forget about my bad luck for a little while.

CHAPTER TEN

I wished Kara's chant had helped me get a good sleep that night, but it didn't. I fell asleep right away, but during the night I dreamed about the earthquake again. This time soccer balls started flying at me from everywhere as the floor shook beneath my feet.

I woke up with a start and looked at my clock—1:16. I closed my eyes and tried to go back to sleep, but my heart was still pounding from the dream, and I couldn't. I kept opening my eyes and looking at the clock. 1:33. 2:07. 2:59. 3:12 . . . When I finally did fall asleep, it felt like my alarm went off just seconds later.

"Did you floss this morning, Devin?" Maisie asked me cheerfully as she dug into her bowl of cereal.

"No," I grumbled, and grabbed a protein bar off the counter.

"Devin, you look so tired!" Mom said. "Have you been staying up past your bedtime?"

"No," I said. "Just a bad dream." And then I yawned.

This was the second night in a row when I hadn't slept well. Which explained what happened next, but it didn't make me feel any better about it.

My first period class was algebra with Mrs. Johnson. I was pretty good at math, so when I'd first come to Kentville, I'd gotten placed in algebra with mostly eighth graders, even though I was only in seventh grade. At first it was awkward, but then I realized that Cody, who's also in seventh grade, was in my class too. And so was Grace, my co-captain on the Kicks.

When I got to class that Monday morning, I felt like I couldn't keep my eyes open—and I didn't. One minute I was listening to Mrs. Johnson talk about polynomials and exponents, and then the next moment I heard her saying, very loudly, "Devin! Head up from your desk, please!"

I started awake and heard some kids laughing.

Oh no, I thought, mortified. I had fallen asleep in class!

Cody looked at me, shaking his head and smiling. I wanted to dive under the desk! Thankfully, Mrs. Johnson didn't make a big deal out of it and kept talking.

There was no chance of me falling asleep in class after that, because I was so freaked out by what had happened that my adrenaline was pumping and my right foot was tapping on the floor. When the bell rang, Mrs. Johnson stopped me on the way out.

"Are you feeling well, Devin?" she asked.

"Fine," I replied. "Just didn't get much sleep last night. Sorry about that."

She shook her head. "You kids, up all night texting your friends."

That wasn't the reason, but I didn't bother to explain. I just raced for my next class and promised myself I wouldn't fall asleep again. Luckily, I was with seventh graders for the rest of my classes, so nobody knew what had happened—or so I thought.

I was entering the cafeteria when Steven walked up to me. We hadn't really talked in a few days, because he'd been walking Hailey to English class ever since her first day. So I was glad to see him.

"Hey, Devin," he said. "Heard you had a nice nap in Mrs. Johnson's class."

A couple of boys behind him heard and laughed. I knew he wasn't being mean, just teasing me a little. But it hit me the wrong way. My eyes started welling up with tears.

Steven noticed. "Don't stress about it," he said quickly. "Her voice could put anybody to sleep."

"Thanks," I said, and then I hurried away. Talk about mortifying! First falling asleep in class, and now practically crying in front of Steven! What was wrong with me?

I sat down at the table next to Jessi, put down my lunch

bag—and then I started to cry for real just as Zoe, Emma, and Frida walked up.

"Oh my gosh, Devin, what's wrong?" Emma asked, sitting down next to me.

"Nothing," I said. "Or maybe everything. I don't know."

"Is it the soccer thing?" Jessi asked.

"It's that, and so much more," I said, and then everything came spilling out of me—my three cavities, not sleeping, losing my soccer mojo, and not being sure why Steven wasn't talking to me so much anymore.

"And then not only did I fall asleep in class, but when Steven asked me about it, I practically started sobbing all over him!" I said. "I'm a mess!"

"Poor Devin!" Emma cried, reaching over to hug me.

"Group hug!" Zoe yelled, and everyone jumped up and gathered around, crushing me.

"All right! Calm down! We're in the middle of the cafeteria!" I said, giggling, as the hug broke up and everyone sat down.

"Dev, I'm so sorry," Jessi said. "You're always so confident. Like, more confident than any of us. I had no idea you were feeling this way."

"It's because Devin keeps her feelings locked inside," Frida said, putting her hand in front of her face. "Her confidence is a mask."

I groaned. "Really, Frida?"

"I don't think it's a mask," Zoe said. "Devin, you are

really confident. It's just that now your confidence is shaken. So as your friends, we need to help you get it back."

"Yeah, we'll be the Devin Confidence Squad!" Emma said, high-fiving Zoe.

I laughed. "So how, exactly, will you help me get my confidence back?"

"I don't know!" said Emma cheerfully. "But we'll figure it out!"

"Well, we can start by sticking together," Zoe said. "Since we don't have soccer practice today, I'll come help you guys with Maisie's team practice."

"Me too," said Jessi quickly.

I thought about that. "Well, I was kind of thinking of having a Maisie-free day, but since you guys are all going to be there . . ."

"That's the spirit!" Emma cheered.

She held up her water bottle, and we all lifted up our beverages and touched them together. I might have lost confidence about a lot of things, but I was confident in one thing: I had the best friends a person could ever want.

CHAPTER ELEVEN

I managed to stay awake for the rest of the afternoon, all the way through English class. And I was so embarrassed about almost crying in front of Steven that I was sort of relieved when Steven walked Hailey to English class. I wasn't ready to face him just yet.

After school I went home to change, and then Mom drove me and Jessi to Maisie's practice at the elementary school field. She seemed really happy to do it, in fact.

"It's so nice that you want to help your little sister, Devin," she said.

I didn't tell Mom that it hadn't been my idea to do this. And I had to admit that the reason I had agreed to was to be with all my friends, but it felt good to help out Maisie too.

"Wow, this brings back memories," Jessi remarked after Mom dropped both of us off.

There were eighteen eight-year-old girls on the elementary school field, each one randomly dribbling a soccer ball. Zoe, Emma, and Frida were setting up orange cones on the field to make a square.

"Yeah, I remember my first soccer team," I said. "I started a little younger than Maisie, though. I think I was five. I remember crying when it was time to leave practice. Can you believe that?"

"Yes, I can, because you sleep, eat, and breathe soccer," Jessi replied with a grin. "I bet you learned how to dribble before you could walk."

"Well, for a lot of these girls, it's their first team," I said, nodding to the field. "Dad says they need a lot of help with basic skills."

"What did I say?" Dad asked, jogging up behind us.

"Just that we need to work on basics with this team," I said.

Dad nodded. "We do. But thanks to you and your friends, we have the right equipment to get it done. You girls should feel really proud of that."

Dad was talking about the fact that the youth soccer program at Maisie's school had almost been cut because of a lack of funding. So my four soccer friends and I had put together a big fund-raiser to try to help out. We had raised enough money, and then some, to get the team back on its feet. (It hadn't hurt that Frida's movie-star costar, Brady McCoy, had showed up at the fund-raiser too.) We'd raised enough money to buy all the equipment the girls needed. Dad and some other parents had volunteered to coach the teams, and the program had been saved.

"We do feel proud," I said, smiling.

Dad glanced over at the field. The cones squared off an area about fifteen feet by fifteen feet.

"All right. Let's get this show on the road," Dad said. He clapped and then ran toward the field. "All right, Panthers! Pick up your soccer balls and gather around."

I noticed that the girls obeyed Dad pretty quickly, without a lot of giggling or goofing around. That was a good sign, I thought. It meant they respected Dad as a coach. Emma, Frida, and Zoe came and stood by me and Jessi.

"We've got some extra helpers today," Dad said. "You all remember Jessi, Devin, and Zoe, right?"

Jessi, Zoe, and I waved hello to the girls, and they waved back. Besides Maisie, I recognized Juliet, a little girl with short blond hair, and Kaylin, who had long, brown braids. We called Juliet "mini-Zoe," and Kaylin "mini-Jessi" because they looked like mini versions of my friends. And Jessi insisted on calling Maisie "mini-Devin." We sort of did look alike, even though Maisie's brown hair was shorter than mine.

"All right. Our first drill is called No Toes!" Dad announced. "I want to see you all dribble around the inside of the square. Try to keep control of the ball so it doesn't leave the square. And when you're dribbling, remember not to use your toes."

Dad dropped a ball in front of him and started to

demonstrate. "Start with the inside of your foot. Then the outside of your foot. Then practice with the bottom of your foot, and then your laces. Got it?"

"Got it, Coach!" the girls called out in unison.

The girls ran into the square and started dribbling. They had looks of intense concentration on their faces. Mini-Zoe was sticking her tongue out.

"Aren't they so cute?" Emma whispered.

"Definitely," I replied.

"You five head in there and watch what they're doing," Dad said. "Help them out if they need it."

We jogged into the square, and Emma clapped her hands. "Okay, so inside, outside, bottom, laces," she chanted.

"Inside, outside, bottom, laces!" the girls repeated.

I had never thought about it before, but Emma made a really good coach! Her naturally positive attitude brought great energy to the practice.

I chanted along with them and zigzagged around the girls, watching them practice.

"No toes!" I instructed one girl, and she nodded and kicked it with the inside of her foot instead.

The girls got the hang of it, pretty much, and after a few minutes Dad blew his whistle.

"Great job! Now I think we're ready for some Keep Away," Dad said. He turned to me and my friends. "Girls, please make the square a little smaller for me. And can you demonstrate how this one is done?"

"Sure!" Emma answered for us. We had all done this drill as kids. "I'll defend. Jessi, Devin, and Zoe, you can be attackers."

"And I'll set the scene," Frida said, as the rest of us quickly went to work moving the cones to make a smaller square. Then Frida explained things to the little girls. "Jessi, Zoe, and Devin are the attackers, and they will start with control of the ball. Emma is the defender, and she has to try to get the ball away from them. The attackers must pass the ball between them ten times to score a goal. If the defender intercepts the ball and kicks it out of the square, she scores a goal."

The Panthers looked a little bit confused.

"Don't worry. It's easy once you see it," Emma said. "Watch."

"Oh, and I forgot one rule," Frida called out. "Each attacker can touch the ball only twice before passing it."

"Got it!" Jessi said, stopping the ball that Dad threw into the square.

Emma ran right up to her, trying to get the ball from her. Jessi turned her back to Emma, kicked the ball a few feet in front of her, and then passed it to Zoe.

Emma sped after the ball, but she wasn't fast enough. Zoe stopped the ball and then quickly passed it to me.

I stopped the ball and then made a quick pass, right to—Emma? I was supposed to be keeping it away from Emma! She kicked the ball out of the square and let out a triumphant "Woo-hoo!"

I didn't know what had happened. I'd spaced out, I guessed. I'd been excited to pass the ball and had passed it to the closest player without thinking. What a rookie mistake!

Some of the little girls were laughing.

"Hey, don't laugh at my sister!" I heard Maisie say. "She's the best soccer player in the whole world."

That was awfully sweet of Maisie, and I probably would have appreciated it if I hadn't felt so embarrassed.

"So, um, do we need another demonstration?" Jessi asked.

I jogged out of the square. "Frida, you're in for me," I said.

My four friends demonstrated the drill again, and this time Emma was a little more challenged to intercept the ball. Jessi, Zoe, and Frida completed ten passes and won the round.

"Think you guys can do this?" Emma asked the younger girls, and they all cheered, "Yes!" Then Emma picked Maisie and three other girls to give the drill a try.

I moved away from the action and leaned against a tree.

So much for confidence. The only thing I was confident of now was that my soccer mojo was gone, and I had no idea how to get it back!

CHAPTER TWELVE

When Maisie's practice was done, I said good-bye to my friends and climbed into the Marshmallow with Dad and Maisie.

"Thanks for your help today, Devin," Dad said.

"Yeah," said Maisie. "That was fun."

"Uh-huh," I said lamely, staring out the window. I couldn't even enjoy Maisie acting like a human toward me, because I was so depressed about losing my soccer mojo.

When we got home, I showered, did homework, and ate dinner, feeling blah with every step. The only thing that nudged me out of my mood was a group text I got after dinner, originating from Emma.

Devin, your best friends are cordially inviting you to Pizza Kitchen tomorrow after soccer practice. RSVP ASAP.

I giggled when I saw the message, and then I went down

and asked Mom if it was okay. She said yes, and I texted back right away.

I'll be there. What's up?

Wouldn't you like to know? Emma replied.

I had no idea what my friends were planning, but just getting the text made me feel a lot better. I went to sleep looking forward to the next day, and I actually slept through the night. I felt a little more like myself the next morning.

Not that the next day was perfect or anything. Far from it. Things didn't get annoying until after lunch (where I begged everyone to tell me what was up, but nobody would), when I went to World Civ class. Mr. Emmet handed back our tests on the Roman empire, and mine had a big red 58 on it, just like I'd feared. I knew that was an F.

"Some of you in the class had trouble with this test," Mr. Emmet announced. "I'm wondering if it had something to do with the earthquake the night before. If you're interested in taking a retest, come talk to me after class."

At first I felt relieved. A retest meant the chance to improve my grade! And that thought made me happy, until the bell rang. As I headed toward Mr. Emmet's desk, I saw Steven move toward me, like he was going to ask me to walk with him. Hailey was hanging right behind him.

But I had to talk to Mr. Emmet, so I shrugged and kind of motioned toward the desk, where a few other kids had gathered. Now Steven and Hailey knew that I had failed the test! So embarrassing. I felt like melting into the floor.

Mr. Emmet put me on the list for the retest, and I headed to English. Steven and Hailey were laughing about something, and I felt a pang of jealousy as I took my seat. I did my best to shrug it off. It shouldn't have bothered me that Steven was talking to another girl. I just sort of missed having his attention on me.

Then, after school, Mom brought me to practice. We had a scrimmage, and because we had to divide up our team to play against each other, I got to play the whole game.

I played okay, but not my best. I didn't mess up—well, not badly, anyway.

A couple of times I lost focus and wasn't on top of the ball when I should have been.

"Look alive, Devin!" Coach Darby called out.

I tried to stop being a soccer zombie and made a few good passes, but I didn't score any goals. I had probably failed to really impress Coach Darby.

So what was to blame? Bad luck? Not-so-good luck? Or had I really, truly lost my soccer skills? As I walked off the field, I imagined a poster in my head: MISSING! DEVIN'S SOCCER MOJO. LAST SEEN ON THE PINEWOOD SOCCER FIELD.

After practice Jessi was all smiles as we got into Mom's car to head to the pizza place.

"I wish I knew what you guys were up to," I said.

"It's no big deal," Jessi replied. "Anyway, you'll find out soon."

When we got to Pizza Kitchen, Emma, Frida, and Zoe

had already found us a round table. Tied to one of the chairs was a silver-and-blue helium balloon with the words "YOU'RE AWESOME!" written on it. Emma pulled out the chair and motioned for me to sit.

"You guys are too much," I said as the balloon bounced against my head.

"Well, you *are* awesome," Zoe said.

"We ordered a pepperoni pizza," Emma said. "No pineapple or kale or anything."

I smiled. My friends knew that I still hadn't gotten used to California pizza toppings.

"Excellent!" I said. "So, what is this about? You can't keep me in suspense any longer!"

"One more minute," Emma said as a server came by with a tray of drinks and set one down in front of each of us. Emma picked up her glass and motioned for the rest of us to do the same.

"To Devin!" Emma said, clinking glasses with us.

"To Devin!" my friends repeated.

I was sure I was blushing. "Seriously? It's not like it's my birthday or anything."

"No, but let's just say it's We're Grateful for Devin Day," Emma said. "You have always helped us out when we needed it. Now it's our turn to help you."

"Aww, guys," I said. "You're so sweet, but I mean, we all help one another."

"But you started it," Zoe said. "Everything changed when you came to Kentville, Devin."

That was a huge thing for Zoe to say, and I almost wasn't sure if I had heard her right. I looked around the table and saw Jessi, Emma, and Frida all nodding in agreement.

"You gave the Kicks the drive to win," Emma said. "I thought I was a lousy soccer player, until you figured out that I would make a good goalie. I never even thought of that, but you did."

"You're not just a good goalie; you're a great goalie," I told her.

"And you helped me get my math grades up so I could stay on the team," Jessi said. "I owe you big for that, Devin."

"You don't owe me anything!" I insisted. "I'm your friend."

"And I hated soccer, remember?" Frida asked. "My mom was forcing me to do it, and I dreaded every practice and every game. But you taught me how to make it fun, by imagining I was acting every time I was on the field. It really works."

Emma nodded. "Besides, it's hilarious."

"Totally," I agreed.

"And you helped me, too," Zoe said. "I froze up like an ice cube every time I got onto the field. But you're the one who figured out that Frida could help cure me by teaching me her tricks for overcoming stage fright."

"And now you're a superstar!" Frida said.

"Not a superstar, but it feels so good to be confident on the field," said Zoe. "So I know how you must feel to lose your confidence out there. It stinks."

I nodded. "Yes, it does," I said. "But you guys don't need to thank me for all that! I was all alone when I came to Kentville. I didn't know anybody. You guys came to my rescue, remember? You were so nice right from the start, and you stuck by me when we tried to fix the Kicks."

Jessi grinned. "Well, if you put it that way, I guess we're all pretty awesome."

Then the server brought our pizza, and the smell of pepperoni suddenly made me ravenous. We all dug into our pizza slices.

"Thanks so much for everything," I said after my first bite. "It really helps to hear all this stuff."

"Oh, we're not anywhere near finished with you," promised Emma. "Since you have helped all of us, it's our turn to help you! Each of us has something special planned for you."

"Oh no! More suspense? I can't take it!" I joked.

"I'm up first," Zoe said. "I'll be at your house tomorrow after practice, Devin. Okay?"

I knew I had no choice. That was one thing all of my friends had in common. When they put their minds to something, they didn't back down.

"Okay!" I replied.

CHAPTER THIRTEEN

When the doorbell rang the next afternoon, I raced from the kitchen, where I'd been having a snack after soccer practice. I could not wait to see what Zoe had planned for me!

I opened the door, and my friend stood there in her soccer practice clothes, a stylish messenger bag slung over her shoulders.

She saluted me. "Zoe Quinlan of the Devin Confidence Squad, reporting for duty!"

I laughed before I stood up straight and saluted her back. "Yes, sir!" I said, and we both cracked up.

"So, how's your soccer mojo doing?" Zoe asked as we walked through my house to the sliding glass doors that led out into the backyard.

I sighed. "I've been holding back a lot, I guess. I've been doing a little better at practice, but I can't seem to score a goal."

Zoe's face turned serious. "Remember how I used to be? I was so nervous on the field that I couldn't concentrate, and it affected my playing. But you had confidence in me, Devin, and that helped. And when Frida showed me tips, they really clicked for me, and it worked!"

I shook my head in agreement. "You are a beast on the field now, Zoe!"

Zoe's cheeks turned a little red under my praise. "I try my best. It's such a relief not to be nervous out there anymore!"

She spotted the soccer ball in my yard. "I think I can help you relax when you play," Zoe said. "You've just got to promise me that no matter how silly these things seem, you've got to commit and give them your all."

I gulped. I didn't like feeling silly or stupid. But at least Zoe and I were alone in the backyard. My mom was in her office, working, and Dad and Maisie were at her soccer practice. So there was no one around to point and laugh.

I took a deep breath. "Okay, Zoe. I'll do what you say. I trust you!"

Zoe smiled. "Good! Now, the first thing you need to do"—she took off her bag, opened it, and took out a small bottle of orange juice—"is drink this."

I felt my eyebrows arch as I looked at her questioningly. "Orange juice?" I sounded totally bewildered.

"It's a trick Frida taught me," Zoe shared. "It can help lower blood pressure and make you less anxious. It's something actors who suffer from stage fright use to calm themselves down."

"Okay, so drinking orange juice," I said. "That's not so bad. I thought you said I was going to have to do something silly."

Zoe grinned. "That comes later," she said. "Let's just chill for a minute while you drink your juice."

We relaxed on the grass, chatting about the day while I drank some of the orange juice. When it was about halfway finished, Zoe told me to lie on my back.

"Get comfortable," she suggested. "You can leave your hands by your sides, or put them on your stomach, whatever feels best."

I lay back on the grass and rested my hands lightly on my stomach. I looked up at the bright blue California sky. Fluffy white clouds were dotting it, and it looked so pretty that I began to relax right away.

"Now close your eyes," Zoe said in her gentle voice. "Picture the rays of the sun coming into the top of your head. The warm light is gently moving through your head, easing any tension. It's taking all your worries away. Feel it move through your eyes, your nose, your jaw. Notice any places that are tense. It's okay. Just let the tension go."

At first I felt really silly, lying out in my backyard and trying to picture sunlight washing through my body. I felt my leg twitch, and I nervously began to tap it, but Zoe's voice was so melodic that I began to relax and not feel so self-conscious. In fact, as she kept talking about the light moving through my entire body, I felt like I might drift off to sleep.

When she finally ended at my feet, she said, "Picture all of the tension in your body draining out through the bottom of your feet. It's gone, and you're totally rested and peaceful."

I breathed in and out, slowly and peacefully. I had never felt so relaxed in my life!

"Now picture yourself on the soccer field. You're in the middle of a game. You're surrounded by your teammates and your opponents. The ball is being passed to you."

I tried to follow along, imagining myself at a game. It was tough to do. It was kind of hard for me to be creative or imaginative. So I tried instead to think about a real game. The last one where I'd played so terribly popped into my head. We were once again facing the Grizzlies. Kristin was passing the ball to me, and I was racing to receive it. I froze as I thought about what had really happened. In my eagerness I had overshot the defenders, which had led to me being offsides.

"Now, don't think about yourself or your fear of making a mistake. Think of your true purpose on the field. To be part of a team and to contribute something valuable to that team. It's not just about you. You're part of this great machine. Everyone is doing their part. Don't scare yourself with what might go wrong. Picture everything going right."

In my imagination I was racing to get that pass. I looked around the field and spotted my teammates, saw how we were all working together, whether it was on defense, midfield, or, like me, as a forward. I slowed my pace and backed up, catching the ball with my foot instead of overshooting the Grizzlies' defense. The defender came at me, ready to swipe the ball from me, but I maneuvered around her and saw a clear shot at the goal. I took the shot, and the ball landed squarely in the net, inches from the goalie's outstretched fingers. This time the whistle blew to signify a goal, not to signify me being offsides. My teammates hugged me, and we cheered.

"I did it, Zoe!" I told her, my eyes still closed as I lay on the lawn. "I made the goal and I didn't go offsides this time."

"Awesome!" Zoe said. "Now, whenever you're ready, you can open your eyes and sit up."

I felt just like one of those clouds in the sky, light and fluffy. As I sat up, I stretched slowly.

"I think I feel too relaxed now, Zoe," I shared with her. "It will be hard to play soccer like this."

Zoe nodded. "It's true. You don't want to calm yourself too much before a game, because that nervous energy serves a purpose too. Try doing that exercise the night before a game, right before you go to bed. To get the adrenaline flowing again before we kick the ball around, we can try a stimulating breathing exercise."

Zoe showed me how to do this rapid inhale and exhale. I had to keep my mouth closed and breathe through my nose. Instead of long, deep breaths, I took rapid, quick ones.

I tried, but my nose made a really weird snorting noise as I tried to mimic Zoe's short breaths. My hand flew up to cover my nose. "I sound like a pig!" I laughed.

"Oink, oink!" Zoe joked. "That's what it's supposed to sound like! We'll call this the Three Little Pigs breathing exercise. The goal is for three in-and-out breaths per second. But we'll try it for only ten seconds the first time, before we go back to normal breathing."

I tried it again, this time not feeling as self-conscious about how noisy my breathing was. Zoe and I did it together, taking the quick breaths for ten seconds before breathing normally. We repeated that two more times, and I felt the energy surge through my body.

I jumped up to my feet. "I'm ready!"

"Let's go!" Zoe said. "You attack. I'll be the defender."

I had the ball under my foot and started dribbling it back and forth with Zoe guarding me. I faked going to the right and instead used my left foot to take the ball to the side, away from Zoe. I dribbled it down the yard as she raced to keep up. All the anxiety I had been feeling drifted away. It was just me and the ball. I raced back down the field as Zoe chased after me. I was in the soccer flow again, and it felt so good.

For the first time in a week, I felt a little more like myself again. And it was all thanks to Zoe and the Kicks!

CHAPTER FOURTEEN

Things had gone great with Zoe, and she'd helped me relax so much that I thought for sure I'd get a good night's sleep. It seemed like I might when I started dreaming about being on the soccer field, like I had visualized with Zoe. Everything was going smoothly. In my dream I had a huge smile on my face as I was about to make a goal, but then the field started shaking under my feet. The ball bounced away from me, so high that it launched into the sky. It became a tiny dot before disappearing completely. Coach Darby blew her whistle. "Devin! For losing the ball, you're benched for the rest of the season."

I woke up, my heart pounding. The thought of being benched for the season was a total nightmare! It took me a while before I could finally fall back asleep. Would I ever get a good night's sleep again?

Even though I spent another day at school feeling half-awake (at least this time I didn't fall asleep in class!), I got a burst of energy when I rode the bus home with Jessi. She had a surprise for me but wouldn't say what she had in store. I couldn't wait to find out what it was!

"Mmm-mnn," she said, her lips shut tight. As soon as we had gotten onto the bus, she had pretended to zip her mouth together, lock it with an imaginary key, and throw the key over her shoulder.

"Come on. Give me a clue," I whined in what was a very good impression of Maisie.

Jessi reached up to her lips and pretended to unlock them. "This is a real *test* of your patience," she said, emphasizing the word "test."

Hmmmm. Test. My World Civ makeup test was scheduled for this Monday, and I had to admit that I was a little nervous about it. But I suddenly realized I was about to get some help.

"You're going to help me study for my test!" I shrieked.

A broad grin spread across Jessi's face. "That's right. I'll never forget how you helped me with math. I just hope I'll be half as good a study buddy as you were, Devin."

I felt like a weight had been lifted off my shoulders. My brain had gone on the fritz when it came to ancient Rome, but now I had my very own gladiator to help me battle to victory!

When we got off the bus and walked to Jessi's

house, Mrs. Dukes was waiting for us at the door.

"I've got some study snacks all ready for you girls," she said as she smiled. "Including Jessi's favorite brain food—banana sushi!"

I couldn't help but make a face. Bananas? And seaweed, rice, and fish? I had heard of some weird California food, but this was by far the strangest.

Jessi saw my face and laughed. "Don't worry, Devin. It's not real sushi."

Mrs. Dukes laughed along with Jessi. "All I do is take some peanut butter and spread it on a whole wheat torti-lla. Then I take the entire banana and roll it up. I slice it, and ta-da! Banana sushi!" she explained.

"Yum!" I said as my stomach growled. Lunch seemed like a long time ago. "Sounds delish!"

"Let's go!" Jessi grabbed my arm and led me into her kitchen, where on the table was a plate with the banana sushi rolls, a big bowl of popcorn, and a pitcher of lemonade. "Thanks, Mom!"

"So, those gladiators did you in, huh, Devin?" Jessi asked as we spread our books and notebooks out on the table.

"It was a total slaughter," I said, and moaned. "I didn't stand a chance."

"You've got me now. You don't have to face the gladia-tors alone. Now let me see your notes." She looked at them and raised an eyebrow. "*No soccer* is one of the things that led to the fall of the Roman empire?"

"It was just a joke!" I said defensively. Boy, did I regret writing that down!

Jessi shook her head, her braids swinging as she chuckled. "Of course you did. After all, you do have a soccer ball for a brain. Now let's go over the real reasons. First, the empire grew too large to be easily managed. Think of it like the soccer field. Imagine it about five times bigger than it is now. Our midfielders would become exhausted running back and forth. You'd have a much bigger area to try to connect with passes. And our goal would be five times as big, giving our defenders an even bigger area to guard. It would be completely unmanageable."

As Jessi talked, it all made sense. I liked how she related it back to soccer. I knew I'd easily remember it that way. We went over the other reasons for the Roman decline and started tackling some of the Romans' contributions to the world that are still being used today. Like cement. Yep, the Romans invented that! Along with a lot of other things, which Jessi helped cram into my brain.

I was totally impressed with Jessi. She was so focused and helpful. "Wow," I said as we took a break to munch on some popcorn and banana sushi, "you should be a teacher. You're good! But I have to say I'm kind of surprised. I remember how you used to be more interested in watching *The Real Teenagers of Beverly Hills* than doing your homework."

Jessi got a sheepish smile on her face. "Um, yeah. I totally still watch it! Now I have a study strategy. I DVR the show each week. For every hour of studying, I reward myself with fifteen minutes of *RTOBH*." Jessi looked up at the clock. "In fact, we've been studying for an hour now. Want to take a reality TV show break?"

"I'd love to!" I said. I didn't usually watch shows like that. They were fun to see with Jessi, though. Her commentary was hilarious.

Jessi grabbed the bowl of popcorn, and we headed to her living room to lounge on her big, comfy couch and watch some of the silly show.

"I'll never forgive you for not inviting me to your birthday party, Taylor!" yelled a teenager named Addison with long, dark hair and makeup that looked like it had been painted on. (When I turned eighty, my mom still wouldn't let me wear that much makeup!) She was arguing with a girl who looked a lot like her, thanks to the style of makeup and clothes, except that the other girl, Taylor, had long blond hair instead.

Addison bent over and picked up a small, fluffy white dog that was yapping at her feet. "And neither will Fifi!" she added dramatically. And at that exact moment, the dog stuck its tongue out.

Jessi and I rolled with laughter as Taylor glared at Addison and Fifi. "I don't care about you or your little dog!" she shrieked. "You only want to come to my party because Nick will be there," Taylor added smugly. "Nick likes me, not you. Get it through your head."

Even though I thought it was the most ridiculous argument I had ever heard, I had to admit I was curious about what would happen next.

I wasn't disappointed. Addison, still holding Fifi in one hand, used the other hand to push Taylor into the swimming pool they just happened to be arguing in front of. Taylor came up from under the water, sputtering and spitting out water before she started screaming.

"These girls are crazy! But they are entertaining," Jessie said while turning off the TV. "Fifteen minutes are up. Time goes fast when you're shoving people into pools!"

Mrs. Dukes walked into the living room, shaking her head. "That show," she complained. "I don't know what you see in it, Jessi."

Jessi threw her arm around my shoulder. "It definitely makes me appreciate my friends more!"

"I'd never push you into a pool," I said, then laughed. "Oops, wait. I already did. Remember that one time at Emma's?"

We both started cracking up. Emma had a really fancy house (it was like a mansion, really) with a huge pool with a slide and everything. Sometimes we could get really crazy when we were hanging out there. And when I had pushed Jessi in, she'd been wearing her bathing suit, not a fancy outfit with high-heeled sandals and full-on makeup like Taylor had been wearing.

"For that, Devin, I will not be inviting you to my

birthday party," Jessi said all dramatically like one of the girls on *RTOBH*.

"Then I'll tell Cody that you're secretly in love with your stuffed bear, Mr. Wiggles," I said, playing along.

"You wouldn't dare!" Jessi gasped. "I'll get even with you, Devin Burke." She grabbed a pillow off the couch and started swinging it at me, and before long we were having a huge pillow fight.

"Girls! Girls!" Mrs. Dukes had to yell to be heard over us laughing and carrying on. "Aren't you supposed to be studying?"

We dropped the pillows but couldn't stop giggling. "But, Mom, this is how gladiators used to battle it out. We are studying," Jessi joked.

"How about you get in some more study time, then Devin can stay and have dinner with us?" Mrs. Dukes suggested.

"That would be great! Just let me check with my parents," I told her.

Jessi grabbed me and started jumping up and down. "Stay for dinner! Stay for dinner!"

I called my mom and got the okay. Jessi cheered. "Too bad it's a school night; otherwise you could sleep over," she said. "But we'll get more study time in at least. You're going to ace that test!"

Who would have thought that a study session could be this much fun? I grabbed Jessi and gave her a big bear hug. "Thanks. You're the best!" I said as she pretended to pass out from the strength of my embrace. I laughed, and she slipped onto the couch in a fake faint.

I was starting to believe that Kara's chant had really worked. I was feeling better and better. After I retook my World Civ test on Monday and played at our next soccer game, I'd know for sure if my bad luck was gone!

CHAPTER FIFTEEN

The next night, before I went to bed, I practiced Zoe's relaxation and positive visualization techniques. I wanted to be ready for my Saturday morning soccer practice and prove to Coach Darby that I could be a player she could count on.

Even though I didn't think of myself as very creative, I was in for a surprise. I was picturing myself on the soccer field having everything go so perfectly that I scored goal after goal. At one point I imagined I was running so fast that I started flying! Soon I was soaring above the soccer field. Things got really crazy when I turned and saw that flying next to me was a unicorn with wings! At that point I had fallen asleep and was dreaming. It was pretty cool.

Then the dream got even stranger when Steven and Hailey started flying ahead of me. I tried to fly as fast as

I could to catch up with them, but the faster I wanted to go, the slower I went. And then I slowly sank back to the ground while I watched them fly off in the sky.

It wasn't a perfect night's sleep, but I didn't wake up with my heart pounding, so that was better than the night before, at least.

Saturday morning I felt pretty relaxed, and for the first time in a while I was looking forward to soccer practice. I definitely didn't want to quit anymore. I actually couldn't believe the thought had even crossed my mind—I was no quitter. Yet I did have a little bit of butterflies when I thought about practice. When I'd trained with Zoe, I'd felt like my soccer mojo had returned. But that wasn't quite the same as facing Coach Darby and my teammates. Would I embarrass myself again?

It's only a practice, I told myself. *Give yourself a chance to get comfortable.*

When I hit the field, I felt fluid and athletic, like my old self. This gave me confidence. We had a warm-up, some drills, and then a scrimmage. While I didn't do anything spectacular (like flying), I had a good, solid practice and managed to assist a goal during the scrimmage. Which to me was even better than seeing a unicorn. Well, maybe not quite.

"Good practice, Devin," Coach Darby said when it was over.

I was all smiles when we got off the field, and Jessi noticed. "Looks like you're getting your mojo back, Devin," she said. "And we're going to make sure it stays that way! Your presence is requested at Emma's house at noon."

Uh-oh. I couldn't remember if I had an appointment with the kiddie dentist to fill those cavities, which I was NOT looking forward to.

"I hope I can come!" I said. "I might—"

Jessi interrupted me. "Relax. We checked with your parents, and it's a go."

"So, will you be there too? What's going on?" I asked.

Jessi zipped her lips and pretended to lock them again. Then she waved good-bye without saying another word before she sprinted to the parking lot.

I went home to shower and change. My curiosity was running wild. I had no idea what the Kicks had planned for today!

Which was why I was practically bouncing in my seat as Dad drove me to Emma's house.

"You certainly seem very happy today, Devin," my dad commented. It was just him and me in the car. "Are things going better?"

I nodded. "They sure are! I had a good practice this morning. And my friends are the best! They've been so supersupportive. I haven't felt this good since before the earthquake."

Then I thought of the earthquake again and shuddered. What if there was another one? Would everything in my life unravel again?

Dad noticed the change in my energy. "Tomorrow night

we're going to have our family earthquake readiness party," he said reassuringly. "Before you know it, we'll be like all the other Californians, taking earthquakes in stride."

I let out a big exhale. Even though we had done some drills as a family before the earthquake, I hadn't taken them that seriously. Now that I had actually experienced an earthquake, I knew I'd give the drills my full attention.

"Thanks, Dad," I said. "I think it will be a big help!"

Emma lived in a private, gated community. My dad had to stop at a gatehouse to get permission to drive through. I'd never forget the first time we came here. The guard had given us a map so we wouldn't get lost! Even though Emma lived in a house like one of the stars of *RTOBH*, she could not have been more different. The only drama in her life was her perpetual clumsiness!

Dad dropped me off in her circular driveway, which had a big, fancy fountain splashing away in the middle.

I rang the doorbell, and Mrs. Kim opened the door, a big smile on her face.

"Devin, it's so nice to see you," she said. "Come in."

I walked into the fancy marble foyer. "Emma is in the rec room," Mrs. Kim said. "You know the way."

I made my way through the maze of a house to the recreation room. When I opened the door, it was dark. All the lights were off. "Emma?" I asked as I scanned the room. I spotted the gigantic television that took up almost an entire wall, the pool table and foosball table, plus the rows and rows of DVDs of what seemed like every movie ever made. But no Emma. Maybe Mrs. Kim was wrong and she was in her room instead?

Before I could turn around to leave, Emma, Jessi, Frida, and Zoe all jumped out from behind the huge sectional sofa and yelled, "Surprise!"

The lights turned on, and I saw that the room was not only filled with balloons, but hanging on a wall was a huge banner that said, DEVIN IS DIVINE!

"What!" I said, totally shocked. "This is all for me?" I could not believe it.

"Yes, it is!" Emma beamed. "I'm throwing you a surprise party to let you know how much I appreciate you. I'll never forget how you planned that Emma Appreciation Day when I didn't make the winter league. And how you helped me see my potential as a goalie. So now it's my turn to help cheer you on!"

"Group hug!" Jessi shouted, and soon we were all mashed together in a gigantic Kicks embrace.

"To celebrate how divine you are, dear Devin," Frida said after we had all untangled ourselves, "we're going to be watching the US women's national soccer team game live. And eating all your favorite foods. Your dad even gave Mrs. Kim his secret guacamole recipe."

My dad had known about this too. He hadn't let on at all. I had been totally surprised.

"Let's get the game on," Emma said as she turned on the TV.

"Wait. We need to eat!" Zoe reminded her. "We've

got tacos, guac and chips, and red velvet cupcakes."

Red velvet! My favorite.

"Wow, guys. You planned the perfect day for me," I said. I actually felt a little choked up, that was how touched I was. I had the most awesome, caring friends.

How could I have ever felt like I had bad luck? With friends like these, it was clear that I had the best luck in the world!

CHAPTER SIXTEEN

The next day Mom and Dad had set up the house for our earthquake preparation party. It was a weekend of back-to-back parties, and I loved it! We got take-out Chinese food, which everybody loved, and Dad made a joke when he opened his fortune cookie.

"Mine says, 'You are about to eat a fortune cookie,'" he reported.

"Really?" Maisie asked. "Let me see that!"

She looked at it and frowned. "It doesn't say that! It's boring. It just says if you work hard, you will see results."

"Boring, but true," Dad said. "And I have my own prediction. After we clean up this mess, we will start our earthquake drill."

It started with Mom showing us an emergency survival kit she had prepared, and a first aid kit, and then she put them both on top of our shoe locker in the mudroom so we would always know where they were. Then we walked all around the house, where Dad pretended to be a tour guide, showing us the safest places to be during an earthquake, and the most dangerous places.

"And here in the Burke living room, we have a bookshelf that's bolted to the wall, which is a good safety precaution," Dad said. "But the books could still fall out, so this is not a good place to be when an earthquake strikes. If you're in the living room when an earthquake hits, under the archway is the best place to be. Now, in the kitchen . . ."

He went on like that, sounding like a goofy tour guide, but it worked. The next time an earthquake hit (and I knew there probably would be a next time, whether I liked it or not), I would know exactly what to do. And that made me feel better.

Sunday night I combined advice from both Zoe and Jessi to prep for the retake of the World Civ test. First I went over the notes I had taken with Jessi, which were much better than the notes I'd taken on the night of the earthquake. I studied for an hour, then took a fifteen-minute break to go on my phone and check my texts. Then I studied for another half hour, but that was all I needed. I was feeling pretty confident.

I hoped I could get a good night's sleep. It would help me on the test. Before I went to sleep that night, I closed my eyes and imagined myself in Mr. Emmet's classroom, taking the test. This time I knew the answer to every question. I filled out the test and handed it to Mr. Emmet before anyone else did. As I was walking back to my desk, Steven gave me a big thumbs-up. I drifted off to sleep, feeling peaceful, until I had this really weird dream that I was taking the test, but the only thing I was wearing was my underwear. No shirt. No pants. And not only were Steven and Hailey pointing and laughing at me, but so was Noodles the Clown, who had been the entertainment at my sixth birthday party. It was totally freaky. I tossed and turned awhile before I could fall back asleep.

Before World Civ started the next day, I took a second to again picture myself acing the test, this time making sure I was fully dressed, with no clowns lurking in the classroom.

My thoughts were interrupted when Mr. Emmet spoke. "All right, class. Today is the retest for some of you. If you're not taking the test, please get a head start on reading chapter thirteen."

I inhaled deeply as Mr. Emmet passed out the tests, and exhaled as I looked down at it. I smiled when I saw the first question.

List three causes of the decline of the Roman empire.

I put pen to paper and began to write. I knew the answers! Every one! I was so excited about knowing them that my pen could barely keep up with the words flowing out of my brain. When I finished, I was eager to hand the test in—and I would have been the first one to finish, just like in my imagination—but then I remembered another tip from Jessi, and I used the extra time to check my answers.

I handed in my paper just before the bell rang. I knew I had aced it! I couldn't wait to tell Jessi.

As I walked back to my desk, Steven smiled at me.

"Hey, Devin!" he said.

Then he turned to Hailey, and the two of them began talking as they walked to English class together.

I didn't give it much thought. I was so eager to tell Jessi about the test that I raced past them in the hall. "So, how'd it go?" she asked as we sat down in English class

"I'm pretty sure I got an A," I said, and she high-fived me. "It's thanks to you, Jessi."

"Devin, you had it in you all along," Jessi said in a mock serious voice, and we both cracked up.

There was one more person I was eager to talk to—Kara. That night, on video chat, I told her the whole story.

"So it started with a mysterious text, and the last thing that happened was that amazing party at Emma's," I said. I rubbed my belly. "Emma brought the extra red velvet cupcakes into school today. I need to do some extra laps at soccer practice!"

Kara had a sly grin on her face. "Gee, how do you think they knew that you liked red velvet cupcakes?" she asked.

Then it hit me. "No way! You told them?"

Kara nodded. "Jessi asked me. Your Kicks friends out there really care about you, Devin." Then she looked a little sad. "I wish I could have been there! If I win the lottery someday, I'll fly out and see you whenever I want."

"That would be awesome," I said. "You have got to see Emma's house in person to believe it."

"I know!" said Kara. "The way you describe it, it sounds like something from *The Real Teenagers of Beverly Hills*!"

"Are you watching that too now?" I asked.

Kara shrugged. "It's hard *not* to watch, you know?"

"Sadly, I do," I agreed. "Well, anyway, thank you for telling my friends my favorite cupcake flavor. You wouldn't happen to know what else is in store, do you?"

"You mean there's more?" asked Kara.

"Frida texted me that we have a mystery appointment at lunch tomorrow," I told her. "I'm a little worried about this one. Frida can be so dramatic, you know? What if, like, she hired a marching band or gospel choir or something? I'll be so embarrassed!"

"Well, I think Frida knows you better than that," Kara said. "All of the other things your friends had planned for you were fun. I think you just need to have a little faith."

"You're right," I agreed. But my dreams that night were of a marching band blasting music through the cafeteria, carrying a DEVIN IS DIVINE! banner!

CHAPTER SEVENTEEN

I was on pins and needles the next day when I walked into the cafeteria. To my relief, no marching band or gospel choir greeted me when I entered. But Frida was standing in front of our usual table, looking very serious.

"You and I are eating outside today, Devin," Frida said. "We're going to need some privacy."

"Uh-oh," I said. That sounded ominous.

Frida led me to a small round table in the shade of the school building. We both opened our lunch bags. Mom was making up for all the party food with a salad of grilled chicken, apples, and walnuts, with a yogurt on the side.

"Devin, I'm here to help you with your most sensitive issue," Frida said.

"Which one is that?" I asked a little anxiously.

"Steven," Frida said flatly. "If he is walking another girl to English class, then we need to fix that."

"Well, okay," I said slowly. "I mean, that's kind of up to Steven, isn't it?"

Frida shook her head. "If there's one thing I learned from filming *Mall Mania*, it's that boys are never in control when it comes to romance."

"They're not?" I asked, surprised.

"They think they are, but they're not," Frida assured me. "In the movie there's this subplot where Cassie has a crush on PJ, but PJ gets distracted by this girl named Marnie who works at the pretzel kiosk. So Cassie pretends to like Matt, and then PJ realizes that Cassie is the one he really likes."

My head was spinning. "What?"

"If you act like you're interested in a boy, they get scared. But if you ignore them and act like you like another boy, *then* they're interested in you."

That didn't make any sense at all to me. "But I don't like any other boy. I like Steven," I told her.

"You don't have to actually like the other boy. You just have to *pretend* you like him," Frida explained.

I was starting to think I would have preferred the marching band to this conversation. "That just seems too fake. How am I supposed to pretend I like someone?"

"It's easy," Frida said. "First, all you need to do is talk to another boy when Steven is around."

"About what?" I asked. This sounded completely nuts.

"Let me show you," Frida said. "I'll be you, and you be some random boy."

"What?" I didn't know how to be a boy. I was no actress, like Frida. I knew she was trying to help me, so I decided to go along with it, no matter how ridiculous I thought it all was.

"Just follow my lead," Frida said confidently. "We'll call you Noah."

"Noah, hi," Frida said, her voice switching to a high-pitched tone. "Can you believe all this rain we're having? It's been making my hair a mess."

With that, she flipped her hair over her right shoulder, letting one of her loose auburn curls fall to the front.

I tried to talk like a boy. "Um, it hasn't been raining," I said in a gruff voice. "It's been sunny."

"Devin!" Frida hissed, going out of character. "Just pretend!"

"Yeah, the rain stinks," I said, again trying to use a deep voice. I felt like a complete idiot.

Frida laughed. "Oh, Noah," she said with a big smile on her face.

"Yeah, rain is really funny," I said in my boy voice again. I had no idea what she was laughing at.

Frida sensed my discomfort. "Maybe you'll be more comfortable playing yourself. I'll be the boy, and you be the girl. Remember to flip your hair and laugh like I did."

I groaned. Frida was my friend, and I knew she had the best intentions, but this was starting to be even worse than when I'd made that offsides goal.

"Devin, hi!" Frida said in a deep voice.

"Hi," I said awkwardly. I sat there feeling like a complete dork, until Frida whispered loudly, "Flip your hair."

The weather and my hair. I couldn't think of what to say as I tried to imitate Frida's high tones. It came out sounding like a dog's squeaky toy. Then I tried the hair flip. I had my hair up in a ponytail. So I wiggled my head back and forth, swinging my ponytail behind me.

"No, no, no!" Frida groaned in frustration. "Take the ponytail out!"

"But I like my ponytail!" I protested.

"Out," Frida repeated.

With a sigh I removed the elastic from my hair. Frida stood up and started pushing my hair around with her fingers.

"Perfect!" she said. "Now flip!"

I flipped my hair over my right shoulder.

"Not bad," Frida said. "But you were frowning when you did it. You can't frown."

Of course I was frowning. This was a total disaster. I couldn't believe that this would work. My skepticism must have shown on my face.

"Devin, you have to trust me on this," Frida said. "I was on a movie set. There was a lot of flirting going on. I know what I'm talking about."

Frida had a point. My experience with flirting was zero. Anytime I talked to Steven, I didn't have to think about hair flips or fake laughs. I was just myself.

"Okay," I said reluctantly. "What can I do to make this work?"

"First of all, when you're talking to the other boy, you have to laugh at everything he says," Frida said with confidence.

"Why?" I asked.

"Because Steven will hear you laugh, and he'll think that you think that the guy is awesome and funny," Frida explained.

"But what if he isn't?" I asked.

"Then laugh anyway," Frida said. "This isn't about the guy, remember? It's about Steven."

I nodded. "So, is that it?" I asked, hoping this lesson was over.

"That's the most important part," Frida said. "Give it a try with Steven and see what happens. It worked for Cassie and PJ."

"In a *movie*," I reminded her. "A TV movie."

Frida didn't get that I was criticizing where she'd gotten her advice. Or if she did get it, she acted like she didn't. She was a great actress, after all.

"Exactly," she said solemnly.

Thankfully, that was all the advice Frida had for me, and we spent the rest of lunch eating and talking about regular stuff in our normal voices.

"Let me know what happens," Frida said when the bell rang, and I nodded, but I wasn't sure if I had any intention of following her advice.

I figured I would maybe just try to walk to English with Steven and Hailey, and then my problem would be over. But when class was over, Steven didn't even give me his usual smile or wave. He and Hailey kind of hurried out, and I didn't race to catch up to them.

Then, when I sat down in English class, something weird happened. Finn Jackson, who was also in my science class, had a seat next to mine. He was a perfectly nice boy, and cute in his own way, kind of tall and lanky with light brown hair and green eyes.

Anyway, as soon as I sat down, Finn started talking to me! I gulped. Now it looked like I would have to try Frida's advice.

"Hey, so did you read the chapter last night? Pretty crazy, right?" he asked.

"Um, yeah," I replied, my voice coming out all squeaky as I tried to imitate Frida. When she talked like that, it sounded like tiny bells chiming. When I tried it, it sounded like a creaky door opening.

"Are you getting a cold?" Finn asked.

I cleared my throat. "Um, no," I said lamely. Great. Some flirting. He thought I was sick instead.

During all this, Steven, whose seat was two rows in front of Finn's, looked back at us. Maybe Frida was onto something.

Oh well, I thought. *Here goes nothing!*

I tossed my head way back to get ready for a really

fabulous hair flip. I was so enthusiastic that I swung my head into the aisle, and I banged it straight into the backpack of a student who was walking to her desk.

"Ouch!" I said, rubbing my head. She must have been carrying bricks in that backpack, not books.

"Are you okay?" Finn asked.

"Yeah, fine," I said, so embarrassed that I was hoping a giant hole would open up and suck me inside. Had Steven seen that? I didn't even dare look at him, I felt like such an idiot. I tried to change the subject back to the book. "So, do you like the book so far?" I asked.

I was mentally preparing myself to laugh at Finn's answer. So I wasn't really listening when he replied.

"Yeah, it's interesting. It was kind of sad when Sadie went missing, though."

"Ha, ha, ha!" I laughed, way louder than I normally would.

I saw Finn looking at me like I had three heads. And then I realized my mistake.

"Did you think that was funny?" Finn asked.

"No, no!" I said quickly. "That was really upsetting, and I, um . . . I sometimes laugh when I'm upset."

Finn nodded, and thankfully the bell rang. Out of the corner of my eye, I saw Steven turning to face the front of the class. So he had seen the entire thing. I felt like melting into my seat.

Frida's plan might have worked in *Mall Mania*. And

maybe it would work for a good actor like Frida. But not for me. So my Steven problem was still unresolved. In fact, I felt like it was even worse now!

As I sat there totally mortified, my mind drifted over the previous week. The Devin Is Divine party. How all my friends had taken time to help me. I would live through this embarrassment. My friends would be there for me. After all, they'd helped me learn how to relax. To be confident. And to have faith in myself. I was thinking they'd cheer me up about this flirting fiasco. Then it slowly dawned on me. My friends had already helped me with this! If anything, Frida's lesson had taught me there was no point pretending to be someone I wasn't. I could only be myself. I knew exactly what to do.

As soon as the bell rang, I walked up to Steven's desk, remembering to relax, be confident, and be myself.

"Hey, can I talk to you?" I asked.

"Sure," Steven said, and I was relieved to see Hailey leave the classroom without waiting for him.

We walked out of the classroom together.

"So, I've been meaning to ask you something," I began. This was hard! "We used to always walk to English class together, and I kind of miss it. I guess I was wondering if there's a reason why we don't walk together anymore."

Steven cringed, just a little bit. "Oh, man. I didn't even think of that, Devin. I'm sorry. Hailey's parents are good friends with my parents. My mom and dad made me promise that I would show Hailey around school until she got settled in and stuff. So I just started walking her to class—you know, as a friend. I should have asked you to come with us."

That made a lot of sense. I wished I had talked to Steven about this right away. I could have saved myself a lot of needless worry. "No, that's okay! I completely understand," I said, relief washing over me. "Hailey seems nice."

Steven nodded. "Yeah, and I think she's going to try out for the Kicks next season. Maybe you could help her with that."

I nodded. "Sure."

Steven grinned. "She'll be psyched. Everybody knows you're one of the best players in the school."

I blushed, and then we started talking about other stuff as we walked back to our lockers. Steven even made a point of walking me to my locker and then doubling back to go to his. So everything was back to normal!

"How did it go?" Frida asked, rushing up to me once Steven walked away.

"It's all good," I said.

"Aha! I knew it!" she cried triumphantly.

I didn't bother to tell her that it was me being me that had worked things out with Steven, not me pretending to like someone else. She would have been too disappointed.

And anyway, it was the push from Frida that had gotten me talking with Steven.

My confidence was getting stronger every day. Now I just had one more mountain to conquer—the next Griffons game!

CHAPTER EIGHTEEN

I am on the field. Jessi passes to me. I take the pass and charge toward the goal. The goalie is waiting for me, a look of determination on her face. But I'm not afraid. I kick the ball hard and low to her right. She dives for it, but she's not fast enough. I score, and the crowd goes wild!

I smiled as I drifted off to sleep Friday night, and for the first time in days I slept peacefully until morning. No dreams about clowns, or Steven and Hailey laughing at me, or Coach Darby benching me for the rest of the season. I woke up a half hour before I needed to and went downstairs, where I made myself a healthy breakfast of hard-boiled eggs, along with a yogurt and granola parfait and a big glass of calming orange juice. Mom smiled when she saw me in the kitchen.

"Wow, Devin. You're up early!" she said.

"Well, big game day," I reminded her. "And I slept great! You and Dad are going to be there, right?"

Mom nodded. "And Maisie. Her game isn't until three. So your full cheering section will be there."

"Yes!" I cried, and then I bounded upstairs to get dressed. I was full of amazing energy!

I was changing into my uniform when I felt the floor move beneath my feet. The trophies on my shelf started to rattle. At first it didn't register what was happening.

Then I heard Maisie yell, "Earthquake!" and our family training kicked in. I dashed into the doorway of my room. Seconds later the shaking and rattling stopped.

Dad ran out of the bathroom. "You guys okay?" he called out.

"Fine!" Maisie yelled, and I yelled "Good!" at the same time.

And you know what? I meant it! I didn't know if I would ever completely get used to earthquakes. They were so weird, and came out of nowhere. But this one had ended quickly, and everyone was in one piece. I took a moment to gather myself, and then I went back into my room and finished getting dressed. There may have just been an earthquake, but as far as my confidence went, I was on solid ground.

The game that day was on the Galaxies' home field in Davidson. As we warmed up, all of my teammates were talking about the quake. Jessi jogged up to me.

"You okay?" she asked.

"I'm fine," I said. "Not shaken."

"Good!" she said. "I had a feeling you would be just fine."

We warmed up and did our pregame cartwheels, and then Coach Darby called the first girls onto the field. She had Jamie and Mirabelle start at forward, and Jessi, Janet, Kelly, and Sarah in midfield—which meant I was benched.

Okay, it's all good, I told myself. Coach might not have been starting me, but that didn't mean I wouldn't play later. I took a deep breath to help myself keep calm. Coach Darby kept that lineup in for the first two quarters, and we ended the half at Griffons 2, Galaxies 3. I thought for sure she'd put me in when the third quarter came around, but instead she put Zarine at the goal and replaced Janet with Meg, and Kelly with Courtney. Still, no me.

I was starting to sweat. Would this be another game where I sat on the bench the whole time? I knew I hadn't been playing my best, but I had really killed it at the last practice.

The third quarter ended with a goal by Jessi that tied up the game at 3–3.

"Devin! You're in for Mirabelle!" Coach Darby called out.

I charged off the bench like a rocket and took my place on the field. My heart was pounding. This was it. My mojo was back, and I was ready to prove it to everyone in the stands.

The ref's whistle blew, and the Galaxies had control of the ball. One of them charged down the left side of the field, right past Jessi, and passed to an open teammate midfield. That player passed it to another player, who pushed passed our defenders. Then she scored.

Griffons 3, Galaxies 4, and time was running out on the clock. But the Griffons had control of the ball. Jessi accepted a pass from Meg and then took it down the edge of the field. I dodged a defender and got open, and Jessi passed it to me. I dodged through another defender as I made for the goal. Right before I reached the penalty box, I kicked the ball over the goalie's head.

Goal! Now the score was tied, 4–4. Jessi high-fived me as we headed back to our places on the field.

I could hear Dad, Mom, and Maisie cheering my name, but it sounded like they were miles away. I was hyper-focused on the game. Tying was good. Winning was better. And I had something to prove.

One of the Galaxies took the ball midfield. I ran up to her from the side, catching her off guard. She dribbled a little too loosely, and I got control of the wayward ball and headed down the field. Two Galaxies swarmed me, and I heard Jamie call out, "Devin! Over here!"

I found a hole between the two Galaxies and shot the ball downfield toward Jamie. She stopped the ball with her foot, but when she let go, the ball skidded away from her, and one of the Galaxies swooped in!

Courtney charged forward and stole the ball away from the Galaxy player. A cheer rose up from the Griffons fans in the stands. Courtney passed the ball to Jessi, who took it a few yards and then noticed three Galaxies charging for her.

"Devin!" she called out, and then she passed it to me.

What happened next happened superfast and in slow motion at the same time.

I took the pass and charged toward the goal. The goalie was waiting for me, a look of determination on her face. But I wasn't afraid. I kicked the ball hard and low to her right. She dove for it, but she wasn't fast enough. I scored, and the crowd went wild! It was just like I had imagined it!

Now the score was Griffons 5, Galaxies 4, and it stayed that way until time ran out on the clock.

"Nice work out there, Devin," Coach Darby said. "That's why I saved the best for last."

I grinned at her as Jessi came up to me.

"You did it, Devin!" she cried. "You got your mojo back!"

"I absolutely did!" I said, and at that moment I knew that no matter what happened—whether it was being in an earthquake, or being benched, or anything else that might come up—I was not going to let it shake me!

ALEX MORGAN

became the youngest member of the US Women's National Team in 2009 and competed in the 2011 FIFA World Cup. She was the first overall pick in the 2011 Women's Professional Soccer draft and landed a spot on the US Olympic women's soccer team in 2012. At the 2012 Olympic Games, held in London, Morgan won her first Olympic medal, a gold, with the American team. The team beat Japan, 2–1, in a match watched live by nearly 80,300 fans—the largest soccer crowd in Olympics history. She now plays for the Portland Thorns FC of Portland, Oregon.